A Mulberry Summer

a novel

Reed Blakeney

Printed in Victoria, Canada

National Library of Canada
Cataloguing in Publication Data

Blakeney, Reed, 1928-
 A Mulberry summer
 ISBN 1-55369-092-3
 1. Hate crimes--Georgia--Fiction.
 2. Georgia--History--Fiction. I. Title.
PS3602.L338M84 2002   813'.6   C2001-903929-8

TRAFFORD

This book was published *on-demand* in cooperation with Trafford Publishing.
On-demand publishing is a unique process and service of making a book available for retail
sale to the public taking advantage of on-demand manufacturing and Internet marketing.
On-demand publishing includes promotions, retail sales, manufacturing, order fulfilment,
accounting and collecting royalties on behalf of the author.

Suite 6E, 2333 Government St., Victoria, B.C. V8T 4P4, CANADA
Phone   250-383-6864   Toll-free   1-888-232-4444 (Canada & US)
Fax   250-383-6804   E-mail   sales@trafford.com
Web site   www.trafford.com   TRAFFORD PUBLISHING IS A DIVISION OF TRAFFORD HOLDINGS LTD.
Trafford Catalogue #01-0494   www.trafford.com/robots/01-0494.html

10   9   8   7   6   5   4

Editorial Comment

Deborah Jones
Diana Bradford
Reida McCutchen

Jacket Photography

Penelope Hale

Copy Editing

Linda Wade
Rhonda Jordan

For Donna Rosalie Blakeney
wherever your light still shines

Author's note

On July 25, 1946, four black citizens, two male and two female, were executed by a mob at Moore's Ford Bridge over the Appalachee river in Walton County, Georgia. They were shot hundreds of times in broad daylight by 20 to 25 white men armed with pistols, rifles, shotguns and even a machine gun.

The murders were never solved, but the current Governor of Georgia has ordered a new investigation.

That tragedy really happened.

The story you are about to read did not. A series of articles about the actual killings appeared in the *Walton Tribune* published in Monroe, Georgia, and they became the inspiration for this tale, which is total fiction.

There were no factual answers back then and there are none in this accounting. All of the characters and events in *A Mulberry Summer* are fictional. There was never a judge Spencer Vinings Tolliver, or a Mattie Lou Herndon, or a Birdie Lee Johnson, or a Billy James Bradley—but there could have been people like them.

Chapter 1
1945

The state road to Mulberry, Georgia wasn't paved in 1945. It ran north from Social Circle, and its red dust rose in a cloud beneath the wheels of the Hudson automobile. The dust whirled over the fence posts and settled on the cotton plants in the fields on either side of the road and the slender black man at the steering wheel loved every minute of it.

Birdie Lee Johnson was proud of the automobile. The car was big and red and hung close to the ground. He left the front windows down and caught the fresh air before it blew into the dust cloud at the rear. Even so, there was a fine residue of powder on the part of his face that wasn't shielded by the brim of his fancy straw hat.

Birdie Lee had come home from the war, and he had $1,200 that had accumulated from his army paychecks that he had mailed home. His mama had put it in the Farmer's Bank for Birdie Lee and he had withdrawn $600 of it to buy the used car.

He hadn't gotten a job, but he didn't need one just yet. What Birdie Lee needed right now was rest and relaxation. He needed to drink moonshine whiskey and chase sweet women. The war was past history and he didn't need to remember it.

He did keep the Purple Heart medal on his dresser though. It was the only thing he had ever won and he didn't want to remember that he got it by being stupid enough to expose his butt to a Kraut battery while pulling a wounded buddy back into a foxhole.

Birdie Lee had always looked after number one and this departure from normal conduct had earned him a machine gun slug in his left thigh and a Purple Heart. He kept it to remind himself to never put his neck on the line again. Not for nobody. All that propaganda about fighting for liberty and democracy was bullshit as far as he was personally concerned.

Fanny's Juke Joint was two more miles down the road and he covered that in about three minutes and skidded the Hudson across the culvert and into the parking lot with the brakes on and the gravel skittering over the dust and onto the porch.

From his vantage place on the porch, a tall, slim negro man slapped his leg and a big smile showed the gold tooth that was his special pride. "Hot DAMN!" Sly Joe Willis muttered in admiration. "Heah come de hero, fresh from de battlefield an jes SPOILIN' fo sum action."

Birdie Lee nodded. "You got it Sly—spoilin' to whup yo skinny butt on dat pool table in back, an don't think I lost my stroke since the las time I took yo money. I done played some POOL since I saw you, man. Played with some REAL sharks."

"LISTEN to de man talk! Lessee if de man kin play pool ez good ez he talk!" Sly Joe elbowed Birdie in the rib cage and proffered a fruit jar of moonshine whiskey.

Birdie Lee unscrewed the cap and passed it under his nose. "Unnh hunnh! You got some real shine heah, brother." He sniffed his appreciation and tilted the bottle and drank heavily. "I done drunk a lot a BONDED whiskey since I saw you, man—some a them fancy French wines too—but ain't nothing beats a good slug a shine!"

The pool game lasted until midnight, and by then Sly Joe had consumed the entire contents of the fruit jar and was becoming more than a little problem for Miss Fanny. Miss Fanny didn't suffer fools and drunks any longer than was absolutely necessary. She was a very large woman with an amazing torso and massive, thick arms that could clobber most unruly customers into submission, but then Sly Joe was a special case. He could draw a switchblade faster than a cat could lick his butt, and it was necessary to be very cautious in approaching him.

Fanny decided to try persuasion. "Sly Joe—you jes axin' fo' trouble—an you know I ain't gone 'low you to mess up my place. Set yo ass down and BEHAVE fo I calls ol' Sherf Junkins!" Miss Fanny's voice was usually loud enough to quiet any disturbance, but it didn't get through to Sly Joe's addled brain.

Bogart County Sheriff Lee Junkins didn't like to be bothered by trouble in the black community, but he had a vested interest in Fanny's Juke Joint. He would make an appearance if absolutely necessary because Fanny paid her protection money right on time for serving alcohol in a dry county.

Birdie Lee was attempting to drag sly Joe out of the joint before the sheriff arrived, but had only made it to the front porch when the big bubble light on the sheriff's car lit up the scene.

"Ya'll come on down now," the sheriff said easily.

"I'm jes tryin to get Sly Joe home," Birdie Lee explained.

"Well, Sly Joe ain't GOIN home jus now," the sheriff said, "so both a you boys jus step on down here like I said."

Birdie Lee let go of Sly Joe's arm and Sly Joe promptly fell down the steps and onto the hood of the sheriff's car.

"At'll be jus fine," the sheriff said, and he slapped the cuffs on Sly Joe and jerked him backwards, then with a foot on his buttocks he shoved him into the back seat of the car.

"Hey," Birdie Lee said, and then thought better of it.

"Hey what?" the sheriff asked. "You hollerin' hey to me, boy?"

Birdie Lee didn't say anything and the sheriff moved his big flashlight from his belt and played the light up and down Birdie Lee's body.

"Come on down here boy," he said.

Birdie Lee came down the steps and the sheriff grabbed his arm and threw him across the car's hood. He added a pair of handcuffs to Birdie Lee and walked around the car to the other back door. "You waitin' fer a invitation?" he asked, and Birdie Lee came around and got in the back seat with Sly Joe.

The sheriff kept Birdie Lee at the jail until two in the morning and completed an arrest ticket for Sly Joe.

"I ain't putting no arrest on record, Birdie Lee. I know yore Mama, and I know you been off to the war—I want to show you some consideration for that."

The sheriff poured himself a cup of coffee and came back to the counter. Birdie Lee shifted on the hard bench on his side of the counter.

"I was in the war too," the sheriff said. "I was with the marines at Guadalcanal. Where'd they put you boy?"

"I was with the Ninety-Second in Africa," Birdie said.

"I heard about that," the sheriff said, "that was a different war from those Goddamn islands in the Pacific."

"I guess so," Birdie Lee said.

The sheriff poured some sugar in his coffee cup and stirred it slowly, and Birdie could smell the coffee and wished he had a cup.

"Well, the war's over now boy," the sheriff said, "an we got to get back to the bizness of livin' in the good ol' U S of A, an I might add, the state of Georgia in pa'ticlar.—now ain't that right boy?"

Birdie Lee didn't say anything and the sheriff slapped the counter with his big, meaty hand, and Birdie Lee jumped up straight at the unexpected sound.

"When I ask you a question boy, you always give me an answer, and make damn sure it's the RIGHT answer. Is that understood?"

"Yessuh," Birdie Lee said.

"Well, all right then!" The sheriff gave Birdie a big smile, and then walked over and unlocked the handcuffs.

"I'm gonna letchu go on home now, Birdie Lee," he said. "I don't guess you want me to haul yo ass up before Judge Spencer Tolliver?" He paused and nodded toward Birdie. "You jus speak right up now."

"Nawsuh," Birdie Lee said.

"Well, at's fine—guess you kin find yo way home?"

"Yessuh," Birdie Lee said.

Chapter Two

In the fateful summer of 1945, Judge Spencer Vinings Tolliver was 50 years of age, and he had been Justice of The Peace in Mulberry, which was located in Bogart County, Georgia, since 1928.

He had two sons, Spencer, Jr., aged 19 and Michael, aged 18, and both of them attended the University of Georgia in Athens.

The judge had attended Emory Law School and returned home to practice as the opportunity presented and to manage the farm his family had occupied since before the Civil War. His family connections reached into the governor's mansion and all the way to the United States House of Representatives.

Generally speaking, the law, in the town of Mulberry, was whatever interpretation Spencer Vinings Tolliver chose to place on it. Cases brought before his court were not appealed to a higher court.

His tenant farmers lived in comfortable housing for the times, and it was a matter of pride to Spencer that all buildings and grounds must be kept in good repair. Every tenant was obliged to trade at Spencer's commissary for food and clothing staples. Credit was extended until the harvest and deducted from the revenues due the tenant.

Judge Spencer Tolliver set his sights, early on, in the direction of the daughter and only child, of James Wilson Crocket. Crocket owned half of the acreage in Bogart County. His holdings included the cotton gin, the cotton mill, the fertilizer plant, and hardware store. The daughter, Myra Beth, was impressed with the young lawyer, and they were married in the spring of 1925.

The following year, her parents, James and his wife Dorothy, were killed in an automobile/train wreck at a crossing in Dublin, Georgia, and their daughter became immediate heir to the family fortune. During the course of the next three years, Myra bore two sons to Spencer Tolliver before succumbing to tuberculosis.

She was not known to be a happy woman, and was in fact so reclusive that many of the county residents were unaware of her illness until the funeral announcement in the *Atlanta Journal.* After that, judge Tolliver devoted all waking hours to the betterment of the family estate and the rearing of his two sons. A more devoted father would have been hard to find.

And so, Mulberry, Georgia, became his private fiefdom, with two separate communities of employees based on skin color. Some distinction was made in the work assignments. The whites worked in his cotton mill, and the blacks worked on his farm.

He controlled the lives and affairs of his employees, both white and black, in a very literal way. A case in point involved the arrest of one of Spencer's Negroes for the crime of murder. The man was accused of stabbing another black man to death in a fight over a female at a club in Athens, Georgia, twenty miles from Mulberry.

Spencer Tolliver got into his black, 12 cylinder Packard and drove to the jail and ordered the release of the prisoner, although he had no jurisdiction in the city of Athens nor in Clarke County. The man was released into Spencer's custody and brought back to his wife and family.

The fact was, Georgians had always respected the power of the privileged, respected the landed aristocracy, before and after the Civil War, and a different set of rules applied to the privileged.

Judge Tolliver had been a strong supporter of Governor Eugene Talmadge since the days when Talmadge was Agriculture Commissioner, and he had even had his picture made with the Governor and President Roosevelt in front of the post office in Mulberry. The strange turn of events in Georgia politics that resulted in Herman Talmadge assuming his father's office of governor was entirely supported by the judge.

The new Bogart State Park, built by the Civilian Conservation Corps, was a direct result of the memorable visit of the President and the Governor. The judge actually had a personally signed letter of appreciation from the President, and he kept the letter with other valuable papers in a wall safe in his study. The picture hung in the entrance foyer of the judge's white columnar mansion along with citations for the judge's performance on the Selective Service Board and various bond sales drives he had promoted.

The judge had reservations about Harry Truman's strong civil rights stance. He saw this as a character flaw resulting from Truman's selfish desire to garner the black vote. He agreed with Senator Theodore Bilbo, of Mississippi, that "every red-blooded white man should use any means to keep the niggers away from the polls."

President Franklin D. Roosevelt had died on April 12, 1945, and Harry Truman had been sworn in as president, but the judge had decreed that the Georgia flag and the American flag would remain at half mast on the county courthouse until July 4th, in honor of the deceased President.

Judge Tolliver devoted himself to rearing his boys, but he needed good help. When his wife became ill, he had realized that a live-in nurse and housekeeper was essential. He didn't want an ignorant farm or mill worker living in his house.

Mattie Lou Herndon had come with good recommendations from a Tolliver cousin in Alabama. The cousin knew Mattie Lou's family in Opelika, Alabama, and knew that Mattie Lou had just gotten her diploma from the famous negro college at Tuskegee. The judge had no objection to having an educated black servant living in his house, and so he met her at the big Atlanta train station, prepared to buy a return ticket for her if she didn't look right.

Mattie Lou Herndon looked exactly right with her light coloring and refined features. The judge noted her erect carriage and the somewhat haughty tilt to her chin as she dismounted from the train. He almost offered to carry her bag before he caught himself, nodded, and informed her that he was the prospective employer.

They talked briefly in the lobby of the station, the judge setting forth the duties that he required, and Mattie, in turn, accepting the responsibility, and informing the judge that she would require a salary commensurate with that of a registered LPN. The judge didn't hesitate and sent the cousin a Western Union message that he would accept Mattie as his wife's companion and housekeeper.

When the judge's wife passed away, he invited her to stay on and help with the boys. She was indispensable. He found her quick wit and intelligence a delight, and during the ensuing months, he offered her some of the best books in his library. She read Hemingway's *A Farewell to Arms,* and Faulkner's *The Sound and the Fury.*

Oftentimes, when the meal was finished and the boys were in their bedrooms, he invited Mattie to sit with him in the library and listen to Jessica Dragonette or Rudy Vallee on the big Zenith cabinet radio.

She was permitted to visit her family in Opelika, but they were not permitted to visit her in Mulberry, and in time, the visits to her family became less and less frequent. Spencer Tolliver and his two young sons became her life's work.

The judge entertained frequently at the mansion and Mattie Lou, in her starched white dress and cap made a distinctive and favorable impression on the guests. A prominent Democratic Party official was not invited back to the mansion though, after Mattie told the Judge the official had propositioned her.

The judge rarely drank hard whiskey, but recognized the negotiating value of alcoholic beverages, especially during prohibition, and so he kept a stocked wine cellar, fermented from grapes on the estate by his black tenant, Pike Edwards, who had a certain proficiency in the production of wine and moonshine whiskey. Over time, Spencer and Mattie would enjoy a glass of wine in the evening.

There was a June evening in 1928, that changed her life forever. The judge had just received a new record for the phonograph in the morning mail. It was George Gershwin's "Rhapsody in Blue." He placed it carefully on the phonograph and listened with his eyes closed as the sultry opening strains of "Rhapsody" filled the room.

Silently, to avoid interruption, Mattie slipped into the room, and the judge was immediately aware of her presence. He opened his eyes and beckoned to her, and she hesitantly came forward. The judge opened his arms and embraced her, and Mattie was too startled to protest. And then they were moving together to the music, and she was mesmerized by the moment, dancing as she had not done since her last days at Tuskeegee and shivering in the emotional high that had come upon her.

The dance ended, the judge still holding her in his arms. She heard him sob and she was instinctively compassionate. And then his lips touched hers and electricity swept through her body. She could offer no resistance as he swept her up in his arms, crossed the foyer, and opened the door to his bedroom.

Chapter Three

They had a game they played sometimes when the outside world was blanketed with night. It was childlike in its simplicity, and it was wonderfully sweet and tender. "Please call me Vinny," the judge would whisper to Mattie Lou Herndon, and he was no longer the ruler of the daytime. He was a young boy, whose mother had referred to him by that name, which was a play on words for her maiden name of Vinings.

That boy had not a care in the world so long as his mother was nearby, but he was very often fearful in the presence of his father. He had always the need to "measure up" in his father's eyes, and he never felt that he could quite reach the mark that was established for him.

Mattie kept the memory of that first time, when the music danced in her head, and she was young and innocent of the ways between men and women. The judge had taken her in his arms and kissed her full on the mouth, and her body had responded to him, had been helpless in its need for him.

Mattie knew in her heart that he cared for her. He showed that in many ways, being generous to her, and in all the years after his wife's death he never courted another woman or entertained another woman in his house. She also knew that the tender moments were played out on a stage, that it was absolutely necessary to have an artificial world where color did not exist before they could come together as a man and woman should do. She had the persona named "Vinny" in the night.

What was artificial to the judge was very real to Mattie. She unquestionably loved the man who ruled her life and the lives of all the people in his employ. She knew also the dark side of him, the merciless autocrat who did not permit disobedience or argument.

She remembered also the day that she deduced that she was pregnant. She kept it a secret for several weeks and then fearfully revealed the news to the judge, convinced that he would discharge her and send her back to Opelika. Once the secret was out, however, there was no question in her mind about having the baby.

On a cold February morning in 1929, the passenger train from Savannah, unloaded passengers at the Covington, Georgia station. Among them, a slender black woman in a plain gray wool coat, clutching a small suitcase in one hand and a bundled up baby in the other. She looked furtively about the station, then spied the black man she was looking to see. Pike Edwards moved forward and, nodding his head respectfully, reached for the suitcase.

"Mornin', Miss Mattie," he said.

"Good morning, Pike. Did you have any car trouble today?"

"Sho did, Miss Mattie, dis ol' car got its own way a'doin' sometimes. I jes has to tinker wid it sum."

"I hope the windows still close," Mattie said.

"Yes'm they do an it's a good thang, wind blowin lak it tiz"

He walked Mattie toward the old Peerless motorcar that he had inherited from the father of Judge Spencer Tolliver. He positioned the bag in the luggage compartment and opened the door to the rear seat. Mattie quickly climbed inside. Old Pike was in the act of closing the door when a voice hailed him from the station. A porter came toward the car clutching a baby's knit shoe.

"De conductor say a lady wid a baby wuz on de train, only baby he saw dis mawnin, and he say de shoe mus' have slip off de

A MVLBERRY SVMMER

baby's foot somehow, an he ax me to han' it to ya."Mattie Lou
reached for the tiny shoe, and the blanket that had shielded the
baby's face dropped away. The porter's eyes got larger, and he
asked, "Where de baby's mama?

"I'm the baby's mother," Mattie Lou said.

"Unnh hunnh," the porter replied. "Looks lak you done got
you a white baby."

Mattie Lou slammed the door, and old Pike started the engine. They left the station in a cloud of smoke from the over-rich
fuel mixture.

The child, Darnelle Herndon, her registered birth name, grew
from infancy into a bright, pleasant young lady, but she was in-
visible to the community life of Mulberry. Darnelle showed much
appreciation for the arts and literature, and Judge Tolliver hired a
private tutor for her when she reached school age. He would never
have considered allowing her to attend the Negro school in the
county.

She had a daily association with the boys, Junior and Michael
Tolliver. A reciprocal bond of affection existed between them in
early childhood, but they drifted apart in the teenage years due in
part to the separated schooling and the divergent interests. Judge
Tolliver thought this was probably best for all concerned.

College was a different circumstance. Mattie Lou wanted her
to attend her alma mater at Tuskegee, and the judge made a special trip with Mattie and the girl to inspect the facilities. The
judge came away much impressed with the school administra-
tion and the responsible and respectful attitude displayed by the
students they met on the campus.

Darnelle had a particularly beautiful soprano voice and loved
music from the days when she had listened to the radio with her
mother and the Tollivers in the mansion's library. The judge was
delighted with her singing but placed priority on a practical course
of study that might equip Darnelle to earn a decent living in the
field of education.

At no time during her upbringing, was Darnelle Herndon encouraged to claim a family tie to the Tollivers. She was the housekeeper's daughter, and the subject was closed on that point. When, at the age of four, the child inquired about her father and where he might be, Mattie answered, with a tug at her heart, that he had died in a sawmill accident.

And so the little girl grew to womanhood in a unique environment that allowed both privilege and privation. She was allowed to enjoy the material benefits within the walls of the mansion and the fenced grounds, but rarely had conversation with anyone outside those boundaries. Oddly, she seemed quite content with the arrangement.

In 1945, Darnelle Herndon was in the top third of her freshman class and had adjusted well to campus life. Despite her sheltered upbringing, she was very popular with students and faculty.

Chapter 4

Mattie Lou folded the last of the towels and took them to the big linen closet off the upstairs hallway. She ran the carpet cleaner over the bedroom floors, mopped the baths, and cleaned the boys' shower stalls. The judge came home for lunch, but it wasn't ready, and Mattie Lou scampered to the kitchen to lay out the cold cuts. She had not been able to keep her schedule this morning because her mind was on her daughter.

"I'm sorry, Mr. Spencer, I've just not been myself today."

Judge Spencer Tolliver looked up from his seat at the kitchen table and stopped the impatient drumming of his fingers on its surface. "You don't look sick Mattie Lou. Is this your special time of the month?"

"I'm not sick, Mr. Spencer, not in that way…it's just…"

"It's just what, Mattie?"

"I really want to see Darnelle. It's been since Easter, and you know she wants to come for the July 4th holiday."

"Now, Mattie, let's not get into that again." The judge frowned and got up from the table.

"Please, Mr. Spencer, let Darnelle come home for the holiday. She has written two times in the last week wanting to know why she has to stay in Tuskegee. Old Pike can meet her at the station in Covington and…"

"Mattie, I don't want to be harsh with you, but you know how difficult this thing is becoming."

"I know, Mr. Spencer, but I also know I want my daughter, and I don't think I can stand it, not seeing her, when she wants to come so badly."

"Well, Mattie, I've got to get back to the mill, so just forget fixing my lunch now. It's too late, don't you see."

"Oh, please, Mr. Spencer, you know you need to eat, and I told you I'm not at all myself today."

Judge Spencer walked over and took her by the arm. He pulled her head down on his shoulder, put an arm around her, and patted her softly on the back. "All right, Mattie. She can come, but there has to be discretion."

"Oh Lord, Mr. Spencer! Thank you, thank you."

"And Mattie?"

"Yes?"

"She can't come to the picnic. You do understand?"

"I understand. We won't make trouble for you, and she can keep right here in my quarters."

"The boys will be coming home…"

"I know that, and Darnelle will be so glad to see them."

"Now that's where we have to be very careful, Mattie."

Mattie sort of doubled up and held her stomach. "Is something wrong, Mattie?" Mattie shook her head, but tears welled over her eyelids. "Now Mattie, let's not do this. Does she have enough money in her account at the Trust Company?"

"Oh, Darnelle is very good with money. She has enough."

The judge took a sandwich from the tray and carefully wrapped it in a napkin. "I'll have to be going now, Mattie. I expect to be home around six, and I'd appreciate it if you could have supper ready on time."

"Don't worry, Mr. Spencer, it'll be on time."

"Well, that's fine, Mattie. That's just fine. The judge lifted his seersucker jacket from the back of the chair and walked down the hallway to the front entrance. He inspected the flowerbeds on either side of his path. It was apparent the yardman had not watered them during the morning as he had instructed him to do. He walked back inside the house and called to Mattie. "Tell Tim there will be no ice cream for him this evening. He'll understand."

"Yes sir, Mr. Spencer, I expect that he will."

Mattie gathered the uneaten sandwiches from the tray and wrapped them and placed them in a brown paper bag. She called the yardman, Tim, who approached from the woodshed where he had slept the morning away. "Tim, the judge said to tell you there will be no ice cream for you this evening. He said you would know why."

"Ol' stingy-gut judge," Tim replied. "Them flower beds didn't need no waterin' nohow."

"Anyway, take these sandwiches to Mrs. Jacobs, and tell her I hope she's feeling better."

"Yes'm, I'll do that," Tim said. He headed down the path toward the Negro housing but stopped as soon as he was out of sight of the house. He unwrapped the sandwiches and ate most of them.

Mattie looked out the kitchen window long after Tim was out of sight, but she wouldn't have seen him anyway.

"I know how difficult this thing is becoming," she whispered to the empty room, mimicking the judge's words. Then louder, as a sob caught in her throat she said, "I know—oh yes, I know."

Pike was waiting at the station when Darnelle arrived for the July 4th holiday weekend. He shook his head in admiration when the smartly dressed young lady stepped down to the platform. Two white taxi drivers vied with each other to gain her attention, but when old Pike approached, and the lady gave him an affectionate hug, they looked at each other in disgust, and one of them expressed their mutual astonishment, "Well I'll be Goddamned if she ain't huggin' a nigger!"

Darnelle didn't express any emotion other than a big smile for old Pike. He walked with her to the twin six Packard and put her baggage in the back seat. Darnelle had always ridden in the front passenger seat when Pike was driving.

"Dis put me in mind a anutha time," he said, "but it wuz col' and rainy den, an it wuz yo mama gittin off de train. She wuz holdin you in her arms so tight an den a porter, he come brangin yo little shoe an…" Pike stopped, remembering the porter's astonished expression when he saw the child's coloring. "Lawd, how time do fly, Miss Darnelle—but we better git you home to Miss Mattie. She be gittin ready fo de picnic."

"What sort of picnic, Pike?"

"Well, de judge say now dat de war be ovah an freedom done here we ought to be havin' a big celebration dis 4th o' July. He inviting some big political men frum de state cap'tal an a congress frum Washin'ton.

"That would be a congressman, Pike," Darnelle said.

"Yas'm, dat's whut I say."

Mattie Lou had just removed another batch of rolls from the oven when she heard the Packard roll into the graveled driveway. She almost threw the rolls from the baking pan in her haste to reach the back door. "Oh Baby! My Baby!" she cried joyously, and the women ran to embrace each other. After the long hug, Darnelle stepped back a few steps, leaned into the back seat of the car, lifted a hatbox from seat, and handed it to Mattie.

"It's for you, Mama," she said. "I saw it in the window at Tenenbaum's Department Store, and I knew it was for you." Mattie placed the hat over the white starched cap, and it stuck up in the air like a small umbrella. She did a small dance on the driveway, and the women laughed and hugged each other again. "Tell me about the picnic, Mama," Darnelle said. At the sound of the word "picnic," Mattie's joyous smile faded, and she began fidgeting with her apron.

"Well, it's for important folks, honey. Not for us. You know the judge—he has certain political obligations…"

Darnelle walked over, and kissed her mother's check. Her ready smile relieved her mother's worried countenance. "The picnic is for white folks. That's what we're saying, isn't it, Mama?" Mattie Lou nodded, and Darnelle gave her a little hug. "Well, let's get this old picnic started," she said. Then, they walked side-by-side, Darnelle's arm around her mother, into the house.

Darnelle sliced the hams that had come in from the pits by the woodshed and had barbecued all night over a slow fire. She placed a slice over a piece of bread and tested the result with a hungry mouthful. "Oh Mama, that's GOOD! I've been missing Pike's barbecuing the worst way, and I just don't know why the judge has been so insistent that I stay in Tuskegee for the summer."

"The boys are here for the summer, baby" she said.

"So…is there some special significance, or what? Junior and Michael and I have spent summers together for God knows how man…"

"It's not the same now, Darnelle. The judge thinks…well, he thinks…Michael… has more than a casual interest in you."

"What in God's name are you talking about?"

"Don't use God's name in vain," Mattie answered.

"Is that ALL you have to say, Mama? 'Don't use God's name in vain?' Why, I can't believe I'm hearing this from you."

Mattie's face clouded, and her lips trembled now. "There are things the judge feels…that are hard to define," she said.

"Oh. Do you think he's afraid I might seduce my brother, Mama? Is that what's bothering His Honor?"

Mattie gasped, and the lemons dropped from her hand. She clutched at the sink top.

"MAMA! For God's sake, Mama, do you think I don't know who my real father is? Don't you think by this time that a child can sense the father's presence in this house? Oh, yes, I know that the autocratic member of the white judiciary is my father. It's time we faced up to the facts of life. I'm 17 years old now, Mama."

Mattie reached for her daughter's shoulders, looked her squarely in the eyes, her voice had a pleading quality," Please, baby try to understand."

Darnelle made an effort to laugh. "Heck, Mama, don't get yourself all upset. I've known that I could claim only one parent since I was ten. Quite frankly, that one parent is better than most folks get with two, so quit that blubbering, and let's get the cakes in the oven!"

Chapter 5

Early on the morning of July 4, 1945, Judge Spencer Tolliver had the American and Georgia flags raised to full height on the terraced lawn outside the mansion. There was still a month to go in the war with Japan, but he had no doubts about the outcome. Sheriff Lee Junkins and his two deputies arrived shortly thereafter, and Spencer showed them the parking areas laid out in the pasture for the guests. The lawmen would direct traffic and park the cars for the government officials.

The judge's 4th of July picnics had been legendary before the war, and he intended his one to be the best ever. The hard work that went into the preparations made everything look easy to the visitors. Among the distinguished guests would be four members from the State House of Representatives, and Congressman Mark McDougald from Washington, D.C.

The tables and chairs were set up on a flat stretch of lawn under large, open tents to protect them from any unexpected thundershowers. There was a country music band from Ellijay. They had done radio shows and had a couple of appearances on the Grand Old Opry and were as close to being celebrities as the folks would ever see.

Negroes were not invited, of course, except for Pike Edwards, who directed the barbecue crew, and the women in the serving line. It was a holiday, however, and the Negroes were free to entertain themselves in such recreational pursuits as might be available to them. Most of them had their own barbecues going in their back yards, and the fishing was good in the Appalachee River. Mattie Lou Herndon welcomed the chance to visit with her daughter away from the crowd. She had done her part by baking cakes, and she would supervise the cleanup crew once the picnic was over. She and Darnelle spent the morning talking about school and clothes and music.

The baseball game started at 2:00 p.m., the Mulberry Lintpickers playing a team from the Chattahoochee Valley. The Valley Boys were tough, seasoned veterans of the game and could have easily competed in the minor leagues. The bottom of the ninth inning showed the judge's team down by two runs, but there was a runner on second base, and he had an ace at the batter's box. The ace was a man named "Mutt" Shelton. He was a giant of a man and distinctly retarded, but he could hit a baseball out of the county. The pitcher for the Valley Boys threw a slider, and Mutt fanned the air for a strike. The next pitch was an outside curve, and Mutt missed again. The locals groaned and urged Mutt to hit the ball.

Mutt took a determined stance; the pitcher shrugged off the catcher's signal, and they communicated back and forth in sign language until the crowd got impatient and insisted the pitcher throw the ball. Which he did, a straight over- the- plate fastball that came at Mutt like a Central of Georgia freight train. Mutt connected with the ball, and there was a moment of awed silence as the ball sailed high into the air over the crowd and over the little creek below the fence line. The Mulberry supporters cheered industriously as the tying run crossed the plate. The judge was exultant and made a mental note to increase Mutt's janitorial pay at the mill.

The crowd shifted now to the food tents and to the elevated platform at the end. The smell of baked beans and barbecue permeated the air. The judge mounted the platform and announced the speakers for the event.

Congressman Mark McDougald was the last speaker before the meal would begin. He had been imbibing heartily from a gallon of Pike's best distilled spirits. He hadn't planned a long speech, but by the time he paid tribute to the late President and to Eugene Talmadge, and Judge Spencer Tolliver, the crowd was getting restless. The congressman noticed and hurried to a conclusion. "When I think of the embodiment of the American spirit, I think of Judge Spencer Vinings Tolliver," he intoned, " and when I think of baseball, I'll always remember Mutt Shelton." The crowd cheered, and the congressman closed by saying, "I think it's time to eat."

The judge summoned the country music band to the platform, and they began with Hank Williams' "Cheatin'Heart." Spencer, Jr. and Michael were not fans of country music, and despite their father's urgings to circulate and converse with important people, they found excuses to go back to Athens. The judge allowed them to go, assured that their presence had been noted.

It had long been the judge's ambition to have at least one of the boys go into politics. The most likely candidate was Spencer, Jr. The second son, Michael, was something of a recluse, and to the judge's disappointment, he had to admit he was probably too much like his poor deceased mother to ever be a factor in the political arena.

Michael Tolliver spent most of his time reading. He read books like *Forever Amber*, *The Robe*, and magazines like *National Geographic*. One time he made a trip all the way to New York City to see a play called "The Glass Menagerie" by a new southern playwright named Tennessee Williams.

Michael would do impulsive things like that. The judge didn't understand him, and because he showed no interest whatsoever in farming, the judge began to think that he should possibly switch his course of study to textile engineering. He might, at some time, take over the management of the cotton mill.

Now Spencer Jr., on the other hand, loved the farm and enjoyed hunting and sports. He had an engaging personality. Congressman McDougald once remarked that Spencer, Jr. was a young man with a lot of promise. "I believe," he told the judge, "that your older son…Junior isn't it? I believe that boy is a young man to watch. I'm going to keep MY eye on him, just in case he comes after MY job!"

At the end of the afternoon, the judge was very pleased. The picnic had gone well. It was, in fact, an unqualified success. The congressman put the icing on the cake when he invited Spencer to bring a delegation from The Cotton Producer's Association to meet Harry Truman.

"Listen," he said. "I know you've had doubts about Harry, but he's not a bad fellow, and I can tell you one thing—he's the man to know if you want a federal judgeship."

The congressman took another pull from his flask. "Hell, you come on up to Washington, and I'll get old Harry to play the piano for you!"

Spencer gave sheriff Junkins three gallons of Pike Edward's spirits and asked him to divide it with the deputies. He called Pike over after the crowd had departed. "You did real well with the provisions today, Pike. I want you to take a couple of those hams home to the family."

Pike grinned from ear to ear. "You jes too kind now, Judge!"

"Not at all," the judge replied. "Not at all."

Chapter 6

The Ford Model A coughed and sputtered its way to the top of the last hill above the town of Mulberry, and then, the engine wheezed and died. The young man at the wheel muttered a barely audible "damn," and quickly beseeched the skies for forgiveness. "Sorry Lord," he stated to the empty surroundings." "I forgot I'm a civilian. I'm not an army chaplain anymore. I'm the minister of the Mulberry Baptist Church."

He slid out of the Model A, knocked it into neutral gear, and pushed it to the side of the road. "I'll come back for you later," he said, as he reached inside for the coat to his newly purchased suit of civvies. He rolled up his sleeves and, with the coat slung over his shoulder, started walking the road to town.

He found the incident more than an inconvenience. He was preaching his first service at the Mulberry Baptist Church, and he was nervous already. "Well God," he said softly, "you've got to get me through this the best way you can, because I'm going to look like I've walked out of the creek by the time I sweat through the next two miles."

He arrived at the church a quarter of an hour beyond the call to worship and walked to the altar to the last notes of "When the Roll is Called Up Yonder." The audience looked with interest at the slender, sandy thatched, rumpled figure of their new pastor. He grinned apologetically and nodded to the choir director and the organist. "I have an old car," the reverend Joe Bryant explained, "and it didn't quite make it to Mulberry this morning. I hope you'll forgive my tardiness, but I had to walk the rest of the way to the church."

There were understanding smiles and nods. Judge Tolliver sat stiffly in his accustomed place in the second row from the front and stared at the ceiling. The two sons fidgeted on the bench beside him until he gave a stern look in their direction. The judge had little tolerance for the worship hour but saw it as a civic responsibility and liked to see it conclude on time. He did not like having the new preacher arrive in a tardy manner because it would likely mean a protracted service that would impinge on his lunch hour and throw the balance of the day out of kilter.

"I want everyone to know," the preacher said, "that I am grateful for the opportunity to direct the worship services in your church. I look forward to the time when I will get to know each of you personally. I want to be your friend and caretaker. I want you to call on me whenever you feel I can help in any way. If the choir director—it's Mike Todd isn't it? If Mike will lead us again, I'd like to hear "Standing on the Promises.""

Mike Todd rose from his seat on the front row, then stepped up to the pulpit and shook the new preacher's hand. "I want to welcome you to this church, and I would like to ask that all the members come by after the service and meet you."

The judge made a barely audible moan.

During the week the preacher did indeed keep himself busy meeting the flock, riding a bicycle while the model A was in the repair shop and learning first hand that the community of Mulberry was different in many respects from the little town of Rutledge where he had been reared. The difference, he concluded, was the uniformity he noted in the attitudes and opinions of the inhabitants. Strange, he thought to himself, that a community bisected by a major state highway could have become so insulated to outside influence.

He found himself a room with a bath down the hall in one of the old, antebellum houses around the town square. The land-lady was pleased to have a preacher staying in her rooming house. She usually had a clientele of construction workers for the rail-road or an occasional peddler for the textile companies.

Toward the end of the week, Joe Bryant visited the only other pastor living in Mulberry. His name was Willie James Wilcox, and he was the black minister of the Spring Branch Holy Ghost church.

Chapter 7

"Sit down, preacher," the judge smiled, and Joe Bryant took a chair on the veranda of the judge's big house. "I'll have Miss Mattie bring us some lemonade, or you might prefer a coke or tea?"

"The lemonade sounds just fine," Joe Bryant said.

Mattie came onto the porch in her white starched apron and black, cotton work dress. Joe Bryant noted the intelligent features and the courteous manner of the judge's servant.

"Thank you very much," he said to Mattie, and the judge answered in her place.

"No trouble at all, preacher."

"Why don't you just call me Joe?"

"Well, people call me Judge—because that's what I profess to be. I believe the same courtesy applies to the preaching profession."

"I just thought..."

"Well, no, let's keep to the formalities, if you don't mind." The judge's smile was still in place, but the eyes were as cold as the ice cube in the lemonade.

"I understand you're not married, preacher," the judge said.

"Well, that may change pretty soon," Joe Bryant answered. "I've got to save enough for a marriage proposal, but I've got the girl picked out."

"That's good," the judge said. "We like to think of our preachers as settled, married men. Keeps the mind better focused on the job, if you get what I mean."

"I suppose I do," Joe answered cautiously.

"Well now," the judge set his glass on the wicker serving table. "I don't hold with beating about the bush. I think we need to talk about your position in this community…what's expected of you, and where you can make the best contribution."

"I'm sure that I can benefit from any suggestions you may have." Joe Bryant answered. He was beginning to feel uncomfortable, and it was not exclusively from the hardness of the rocking chair seat. He placed his glass on the table along side that of the judge and turned to face him. "What did you have in mind?"

"I believe the word is 'do' have in mind, the judge answered. "I do have in mind several things, but I'll start with a question for you." The steely eyes bored into the preacher. "What were you doing in that niggra preacher's house the other evening?"

Joe Bryant felt a flush of anger grip him, but he answered quietly, "Why do you want to know?"

"I want to know," the Judge said, "because Willie James Wilcox may be the preacher he purports to be, but he's also head of the local chapter of the NAACP, a communist directed organization, intent on the overthrow of the government of the United States."

Joe Bryant sucked in his breath and carefully controlled the resentment he felt toward the Judge. "You will have to prove that last statement to me," he said. "I don't mean the part about his heading the NAACP but the part about it being a communist directed organization."

"No, I don't have to prove anything to you, son," the Judge stated. "What I have to do is to keep you from making a serious mistake in judgment. You don't want to get off on the wrong foot around here. I'll make it as plain as I can make it. We don't socialize with Negroes here in Mulberry. We don't have friendly social gatherings in each other's homes because we know that's not what God intended us to do."

"You really think God would oppose a mixed social gathering of his children?" Joe Bryant asked.

"Now think about it preacher," the judge came back to formalities. "You're not a stranger to this part of the country. Why in the world would you have gotten it in mind to pay a social call on the leader of the NAACP?

"I didn't think of him as the leader of the NAACP," Joe answered. "I thought of him as a fellow pastor, a member of the Christian community. I have always loved the Negro spirituals, and I had it in mind to invite him to bring his choir to our church some time."

"You had it in mind to do something like that…without discussing the matter with the congregation?"

"Well, I didn't see it as a big deal one way or the other," Joe said.

"You have much to learn, preacher. My advice to you is to move slowly and carefully in the execution of your pastoral duties, and keep in mind your heritage and the heritage of the people you plan to serve. It will just work out better for everybody concerned."

"I'm afraid I don't understand," Joe Bryant said. "What's coming through to me is that you intend me to check with you on any matter that you consider to be a change in the attitude toward segregation."

"Then, you are understanding me correctly, preacher. That's exactly what I expect you to do…until you have gained enough experience to make your own sound judgments."

"Well, I thank you for the lemonade," Joe Bryant said.

"You'd better thank me for the advice as well," the judge smiled, "because I think you can have a good future here in our little town. Bring the intended with you on the next Sunday service, and the two of you come on out here to Sunday dinner." The judge rose from his seat and proffered his hand. Joy Bryant took it somewhat reluctantly.

"There was another reason I asked you out here today," the judge said. "Another reason why I brought up the subject of marriage. You see, I have several properties that the good Lord has seen fit to entrust to my care. One of them is located right down the street from the church. It has its own garden space and a play area for the children that are bound to come. I've been thinking of donating that property to the church. If you like it, you can consider it your new home."

"I don't know what to say," Joe Bryant answered.

"But you will consider it?" the judge asked.

"I don't see where I can refuse," Joe said.

"Than it's settled. You come with me tomorrow, and we'll look it over, then, you bring your finance, and let her look it over. Women always have changes in mind, another thing you have to learn. We'll listen to what she has to say, and then, we'll get it fixed up for her."

Joe Bryant drove away in a muddled state of mind. He had been offered a house and an opportunity to propose marriage sooner than he had hoped to do. He also felt as if he had made a bargain that he would come to regret.

Chapter 8

Sheriff Lee Junkins had been involved in law enforcement for most of his adult life. His first job had been with the state prison system, where he worked as a guard for the chain gangs that cleared the roadsides on the graveled roads throughout the county. The job afforded a marginal living wage, but not enough to support the young wife and two children already in his household, and certainly not enough to support the third child on the way.

He applied for, and was hired as a deputy sheriff in Bogart County. He was industrious and generally cool headed under stress, and he worked his way up to chief deputy by the time old Wilson announced his retirement. He ran for the office, and Judge Tolliver gave him his blessing, which was tantamount to victory.

Things got better for him financially. For one thing, he became acquainted with Miss Fannie Mae Hill, who owned the Blue Goose juke joint in the Negro section of Mulberry. Miss Fannie Mae usually ran an orderly place of business and didn't bother him with any of the usual razor cuts and brawls.

He paid a call on her, soon after his election. Working on his knowledge of the activities in progress at her establishment, he presented the lady with a proposal for her continued operation.

"Well, Miss Fanny," he said, as he smiled in genuine friendliness, "we're all in business to make a little money, don't you think?"

"Lawd, Sherf Junkins, ain't nobody making no money around here, we jes be…"

The sheriff's smile was gone now, and he reached for the handcuffs hanging on the back of his big, broad leather belt. He carefully removed them and held them out for Fannie's inspection. "I don't guess I need to tell you what's gonna happen if you an me don't reach an understandin', now do I?"

"Nawsa, Sherf, I ain't meanin' no disrespec or nuthin…I jes misunderstood is all."

The sheriff's smile returned, and he put the handcuffs back on his belt and slapped Fannie on her massive left shoulder. "You and me can be friendly and avoid any unfortunate consequences I think."

"Lawd, I don't need me no unfortunate…whut you say?"

"Consequences, Fannie…those things that happen when somebody breaks the law around this county. Things like courtroom introductions to Judge Tolliver…things like a cold, flat cot in the jailhouse with nothin' but a sink and shithole for company. Do you get my drift?"

Fannie's features hardened into a black mask, and she nodded her head, her voice weary and full of resignation. "How much you want, Sherf?"

"That depends. You keep up with them whiskey sales…I got a pretty good idea what that amounts to on a Saturday night, an' I'll take just 20% of that. I guess you know percentage don't you? What that means is every damn dollar you stick in that cigar box under the counter, you put two dimes in another box for me. Now if you cooperate with me, things gone be okay. My depities ain't gone come in here bustin' up the place, lookin' for moonshine, stuff like that… Yeah, you cooperate, and we gone get along fine. If not…well…"

"Ain't no problem, Sherf."

"Well, hell…I guess not. Look at it as a license fee, cause that's what it amounts to. Everybody has to have a license to do business—and to sell alcohol when everybody knows that's prohibited...well, hell, that's got to cost a little more...right?"

"You right, Sherf."

"Course I am...right as rain, if you know what I mean. I'll try to drop by...say on Monday evenings. That'll give you time to tally up the weekend receipts, and we'll see how that works out for us."

It worked out pretty good from the outset, and the extra income came in handy when the fourth child was born into the Junkins household.

Chapter 9

"Birdie Lee," his mama said, "you ain't eatin'. You jes messin' wit dat food!" She scraped the food from Birdie's plate into the bucket of pig slops and looked sternly in his direction. "How come you ain't eatin' right?"

"I ain't eatin' 'cause I ain't got no appetite for collards and cornpone, Mama."

"Whut chu talkin', Birdie? Cornbread and collard greens is GOOD fo you!"

"Well, I don't want it. I never did want it, and I don't have to eat it no more. I don't have to eat nothin' I don't want, and I don't care if it's good for me or not, so don't give me no hard time, Mama."

"Comin' in AT THREE O'CLOCK in de mawnin'! I kin see you got some bad ways of doin' now, but you don't talk disrespectful to yo Mama!"

"You gone be tellin' me what I kin do now, Mama? I been to the war, Mama. I seen things you can't even imagine, and I done things you don't want to know 'bout, so don't be givin' me no flack 'bout when I come in."

"You watch yoself, Birdie. Jus watch yoself is whut I say. You be headin' right down trouble road."

"I been on trouble road all my damn life, Mama."

"Don't chu be usin' no cuss words wit' chu Mama."

Birdie Lee crossed the kitchen floor on his bare feet and gave his mother a hug. "Don't worry none, Mama, ain't nothing bad comin' my way. I done been thru bad, Mama. I'm home now, don't you see?"

"You home…but you diffrunt somehow, Birdie. You diffrunt than you used to be."

"Damn right I'm diffrunt, Mama. I got a right to be diffrunt, but I kin tell ain't nuthin' diffrunt 'round here!"

"Don't be using cuss words wit' chu Mama!"

Birdie laughed and slapped his mama on her broad behind, then jumped over the slop bucket in his haste to dodge her strong right hand.

After a few minutes, Birdie came swinging through the house wearing the new straw hat and white linen trousers with a shiny, rayon sport shirt and a duffel bag of clothing.

"Where you goin', Birdie Lee? Thought you wuz gone help me 'round de house today."

"Later, Mama, later. I think I'm goin' over to cousin Leona's and get these civilian clothes let out to fit me again. Didn't know I put on some growth, eatin' that army mess food."

"You coulda axed me to go wit' chu."

"Later, Mama. I got some plans for the day with Sly Joe."

"That good-for-nothin' Sly Joe…you better watch yoself."

"Yeah, Mama."

Birdie threw the duffel bag in the back seat and spun the Hudson around in the dirt driveway, then plowed across the yard and onto the country road to Mulberry.

Miss Leona Jacobs was the seamstress in Mulberry for anybody requiring tailored clothing.. She worked for the whites and for the blacks, and she knew instinctively to modify a dress pattern when the customer didn't appear to be the right candidate for the style. She had been Mattie's seamstress since she first came to Mulberry, and she had made Darnelle's clothing from infancy to her going away wardrobe for college.

Her eyes had been failing her in recent months, and her hands were twisted with arthritis, but she continued to ply her trade for the long list of customers, though at a much slower pace. Mattie tried to check on her from time to time to make sure she was eating properly and to render assistance with the household chores. She felt it was the least she could do for all the years of good service from Mrs. Jacobs. Many of her gestures of kindness were subverted by the worthless Tim, who would keep or eat a portion of anything that was given to him for delivery to the old lady.

The abundance of food left over from the July 4th picnic reminded Mattie that Mrs. Jacobs would appreciate a plate of barbecued short ribs and some of the stuffed eggs. Darnelle was pleased to take the food basket. She hadn't seen Mrs. Jacobs since she left for college, and since she was banned from the picnic area anyway, the trip to Mrs. Jacob's house was a welcome diversion. She noticed the red Hudson automobile in the driveway as she approached and figured a customer was inside, so she waited on the porch swing until Birdie Lee came out the door.

"Have mercy!" Birdie exclaimed, and he staggered against the doorjamb as if he had received an electric shock. "Would you LOOK at what I see in the old porch swing! Whut's yo name, baby?"

Darnelle was immediately offended. "I'm not a baby, thank you very much!"

"No shit! You ain't no baby an' you don't talk like nobody 'roun here. Where you stay, anyway?"

"That's none of your business," Darnelle said.

"Well, ain't you the fine one. I 'spect I could teach you something!" Birdie Lee said, and he grabbed his crotch for emphasis.

"You are a vulgar, ignorant fool," Darnelle said coolly, as she rose from the swing just as Mrs. Jacobs came to the front door.

"Oh Birdie! I thought you was gone, then seem like I heard voices," Mrs. Jacobs said.

"You heard voices all right," Birdie answered. "This here's one smart aleck, high yeller gal on your porch."

"What? Where…on my goodness, Darnelle! I'm glad to see you honey. Just excuse this cousin of mine. He's home from the war and cuttin' up just to aggervate you!" She turned back to Birdie Lee and clutched at his arm, "Can't see too good no more, but I can see you better leave this young lady alone, Birdie. Don't be messin' 'roun her any more or it might be too bad fo you!"

Birdie shrugged her hand off his arm and started down the steps, but his pride was hurt, and he turned around to face Darnelle again. "Don't worry baby," he said softly. "You'll be seeing me again." He got in the Hudson and roared out onto the road in reverse, then changed gears and spun the tires in the gravel.

"Don't pay him no mind," Mrs. Jacobs said. Yet, Darnelle couldn't shake a feeling of apprehension as she walked home with the empty food basket.

Chapter 10

Birdie Lee was disenchanted with his readjustment to civilian life. He had seen a different lifestyle available for Negroes in Europe, and he had to compare the land of his birth with the world that he had experienced overseas. More and more, Birdie was convinced that the system in Bogart County, Georgia, needed changing.

The home turf was more familiar to him; he understood the lifestyle of the black man in Georgia, and he had not been too uncomfortable with it before the war. However, now he had different vibes, and he couldn't find good answers for the questions that dogged his mind. For one thing, why did he have to sit in the balcony at the local picture show? He paid the same ticket price as the whites. It was true that he had more fun with his own kind in the upstairs seating area and often had the better view of the screen, but the question dogged him.

And it wasn't just that. Try going out to eat and you stood at the window for a carryout order while all the white folks and their families gathered in comfort inside the cafes, laughing, joking and enjoying the outing. Yeah, and if you needed to take a shit, you couldn't just walk in the first available restroom. You had to find one labeled "Colored," or just park your car on the side of the road and head for the bushes.

Of course, most blacks didn't have cars. If you made a trip, you rode on a train or the Trailways bus, and you sat in the area assigned to colored—always in the back of the bus. You carried your food in a paper sack and ate on the way because finding food on the road could be a big problem. Many times a restaurant would simply refuse to serve you, period. Some had signs: "No Niggers Allowed."

But the thing that really bugged him was the way the black folks accepted their lot—just accepted all this crap and tried to stay out of trouble—like "yessuh, Cap'n, suh; sho nuff Cap'n, suh," doffing a hat, puttin' on the polite face—like his mama, always telling him he was headed for trouble. Well, damn-it-all-to-hell, maybe he was, but the friggin' government shouldn't have put him in uniform and sent him overseas if they expected him to live the rest of his life like these cornpone darkies.

The way Birdie figured it, the white man's system had gone unchallenged for too long a time. Maybe his name WAS trouble, but he had put his ass on the line for all these same white folks who thought Hitler was wrong for calling Germans the Super Race. Well, they sure as shit thought they were super compared to Birdie Lee Johnson, didn't they?

Birdie went to Fanny's and found Sly Joe playing pool and being pretty agreeable with everybody. Old Sheriff Junkins had kept him in jail for a week last time. Of course, he let him work during the day at the sheriff's farm, cutting hay and putting up silage.

"Yo Birdie," Sly Joe said, "play you a game of pool?"

"Nah," Birdie replied, "I was thinkin' of going to the picture show."

"How come?"

"What sort of a dumbass question is that..."how come?"

"Well, I didn't know there wuz nuthin' playing tonight."

"There's sumthin' playin SOMEWHERE.!"

"Okay, Birdie, let's go to the show."

"Who asked YOU to go?"

"Well, you brought it up, Birdie, but if you don't want me to go, well, you can kiss my black ass!"

Birdie laughed. He suddenly felt much better. Sly Joe did that for him, made him feel better. You had to hand it to a man who could do that.

They ambled out, slid into the Hudson and headed down to the Mulberry Theatre. The sign on the marquee advertised a Gene Autry western, and Sly Joe said, "Hell, I ain't gone waste my time on a ol' Gene Autry movie."

Birdie Lee didn't say anything, just parked the car and started toward the ticket window. Sly Joe followed along because he didn't have anything planned for his time. Birdie bought two tickets and handed one to Sly Joe, but instead of walking to the outside staircase that led to the Negro seating upstairs, he just walked straight into the darkened theatre and took a seat near the front.

Sly Joe stood awkwardly at the entrance, and the ticket agent pointed to the stairs. Sly Joe started in that direction, but suddenly decided to go find Birdie Lee and ask him what the hell was going on.

They both found out soon enough.

The ticket agent called the manager, and the manager went down the rows until he spotted the two Negro men. "You can't sit here," he said. "Get on up to the balcony."

"Why don't you make us?" Birdie Lee asked.

The theatre manager was past middle age, soft and fat, and in no condition to make anybody do anything, but he couldn't just stand there and allow a nigger to talk back to him. "I'll give you two minutes," he said.

"And I'll give you a foot up your fat ass," Birdie said. Sly Joe was very agitated now. "Let's git goin'," he said.

The theatre manager sensed an ally. "That's right," he said. "Y'all move on now and there won't be any trouble."

"My name is trouble," Birdie Lee said.

By now the patrons in the seats in front and the ones behind had grasped the situation. A man in a pair of blue overalls reached in his pocket and brought out a blackjack, reached over the seat from behind Birdie Lee and popped him behind the right ear. Birdie Lee immediately slid down in his seat, and Sly Joe grabbed him and tried to get him to his feet, but Birdie was out like a light. Now, the whole place was in an uproar, and the manager ran up the aisle to the office and called Sheriff Junkins.

Birdie Lee didn't remember too much about the trip to the jail. Once the sheriff and the deputies arrived, he had been summarily batted with a nightstick or a flashlight or something that was hard and heavy. Things got kind of fuzzy and distant, then, he heard angry voices and the clanging sound of an iron door. .

He looked over from the bare mattress cot in the jail cell and saw Sly Joe in the next cell. Sly Joe had a big knot over one eye; dried blood was on his face. Then, the Sheriff came into view between the gratings on the cell.

"Well," the Sheriff said, "if it ain't Birdie Lee Johnson in the flesh!" The Sheriff did not look happy, and Birdie and Sly Joe avoided looking at him. "A hell of a note," the Sheriff continued. "Decent people going to the picture show for some relaxation, and here comes a trouble-makin' nigger down the aisle to spoil the evening. Make that TWO trouble-making niggers…ain't that right, Sly Joe?"

"Nawsuh," Sly Joe said. "I wuz jes goin' to git Birdie…"

"Well," the Sheriff said, "it looks like you boys is always goin to git the other one. Birdie Lee here was just goin' to get you out of Fanny's place last time we met. Ain't that right Birdie?" Birdie Lee didn't say anything, and the Sheriff walked over and kicked him on the shin.

"DAMN!" Birdie hollered, "that HURT!"

"Meant for it to hurt," the Sheriff said, "because you didn't remember what I told you last time. When I ask you a question, boy, you got to remember what?

"To give you an answer," Birdie said.

The Sheriff kicked him again, and Birdie hollered louder.

"No, boy," the Sheriff said, "I tole you to give me the RIGHT answer, and the right answer is that you're a trouble-making son-of-a-bitch!" He punched Birdie in the stomach, and Birdie doubled over on the floor.

"Judge Tolliver will be coming by to see you later," the Sheriff said, and he slammed the cell door and went out to breakfast.

Birdie Lee and Sly Joe hadn't had any breakfast, but they didn't have much appetite anyway.

Forty-five minutes later Judge Tolliver made his appearance.

"I don't think we need to made any formal case out of this incident," he said, and he looked the boys over carefully, then turned back to the Sheriff. "Actually, I think we should keep this whole affair as quiet as possible. No need to stir up the folks in Mulberry or in Bogart County…and I'm sure you will see to it that these boys learn to behave themselves. Are these boys some of my Niggras?"

"No sir," the Sheriff answered. "Birdie Lee Johnson is staying with his mama out on Flat Creek Road. She does laundry for the town folks. And Sly Joe Willis there is a bootlegger, spends most of his time out at Fanny's."

The judge nodded solemnly. "Real upright citizens, I can see. Well, Sheriff I want you to teach these boys that being disruptive to the peace and tranquility of our little town can prove to be costly…and painful…to the perpetrator. I want these boys to work up a sweat. I want them down in my swamp cutting pulpwood for the rest of the week. Now, if that doesn't make a point with these boys, we can think of other remedies, eh Sheriff?"

Sheriff Junkins nodded. "I think we can handle it."

Chapter 11

The judge left for Washington on July 10, 1945, and took two other members of the Georgia Cotton Producers Association with him. They went on the train in order to have more time for conversation and poker playing, and because the judge didn't like to fly.

The boys came back from Athens and finding the judge out of town, took some liberties with his supply of corn whiskey, figuring the judge would not notice or might attribute the shortage to Congressman McDougald's visit. In any case, they got a bottle and put it in the glove compartment of Spencer's convertible and asked Mattie to pack them a picnic basket.

"By the way," Spencer said, "if Darnelle has nothing to do today, she can go on a picnic with us. We had thought about driving down to the Bogart State Park."

"I don't know," Mattie said. "There might be a problem if people saw her in your car at the park."

"Oh, you mean because..." Spencer halted, then fell silent.

"Because she is a colored girl," Mattie said.

"But she's not black," Michael protested. "She's whiter than some of the girls at the University who come from other countries."

"And she's prettier than any of them, too," Spencer added.

"Oh, I don't know…" Mattie fretted, knowing the judge would not approve if he were here. But, on the other hand, he was not here, and Darnelle had been cooped up ever since she arrived. She deserved to have some fun on her summer vacation, and she would be returning to her school in a few days to take part in the Tuskegee Chorale's summer concert tour.

Finally, she gave her approval to the boys, and they called Darnelle out of her lawn chair by the pond. "Put the book away," Spencer called, "and get into a swim suit so you can enjoy the park!"

Darnelle was thrilled at the invitation. she had never ridden in Spencer's new car and had never seen the new park facility. Negroes were not expected to go there. Not that any signs were posted to that effect, but black folks just had a sixth sense about such things.

The outing brought back many memories of their childhood days. They had often gone places together as children, and Mattie's daughter's presence was not a problem back then. People accepted Mattie's role as the nanny, and it was a natural thing to have her daughter in her care. Almost every sentence began with "Do you remember?" They were entering the park before any of them realized; the trip had been so filled with reminiscences.

The park ranger's office was just down the road on the right, and folks were expected to pay a 50-cent parking fee if they got out of the car. All three of them got out and went into the office. Michael got some cokes for the three of them while Spencer paid the fee.

The ranger was a tall, sallow faced man with what appeared to be an enormous emotional burden on his shoulders. He looked them over carefully and accepted the fee while listing the various rules and regulations designed to keep the park in its pristine condition. Spencer assured him that they would observe all the rules of conduct pertaining to fires and litter, then, they proceeded down to the picnic area by the lake. Spencer got the picnic basket. Darnelle carried the cokes, and Michael covered the bottle of corn whiskey under the blanket and carried a battery-powered phonograph.

The CCC boys had hauled in white sand to make a beach for the swimming area, and the limits for swimming were marked off by colored ropes and buoys. There were no other visitors to the beach on this middle of the workweek, and the day belonged to the three of them.

"Oh, how delightful!" Darnelle cried.

"Thank the judge and Eugene Talmadge," Spencer said. "Let's have a little drink to both of them," Michael suggested.

"Are you serious?" Darnelle asked.

"Absolutely," Michael said, and they all laughed. Michael opened a coke bottle, poured off half of it and filled it back to the top with the moonshine. They passed the bottle around, and Michael put a record on the machine. "Sentimental Journey" fell in mellow fashion on the air. Darnelle sang along with the music, and her voice was so beautiful that Michael got emotional from the music and the whiskey and suddenly felt like crying.

"Come on, come on," Darnelle insisted. "Let's all sing."

And sing they did, between long pulls from the bottle. Darnelle was sure there had never been a more joyous day in all of her life.

They went swimming and stayed within the boundaries laid out by the boys from the CCC. The water couldn't have been more than six feet in depth at its deep end, and both of the boys were excellent swimmers.

Darnelle had never been instructed in the art of swimming the backstroke, so Michael took it upon himself to teach her, holding her body afloat while going through the arm pulls in proper sequence. He felt a strong attraction to the lovely girl, and he noted how long and shapely her legs appeared. He felt the lithe and rounded form of her under his guiding arm, and he suddenly went weak in the knees and moved away.

"What's wrong, Mikey?" Darnelle asked.

"I don't know," Michael confessed, "Maybe I went a little heavy on the spiked coke."

"Don't worry," Darnelle said, "we'll just lie down on the beach a while until you feel better."

Shortly, he did begin to feel better and was almost ready to tell Darnelle how he felt when they heard Spencer calling from the picnic area. They soon devoured the stuffed eggs and tomato sandwiches, then stretched out on the blanket.

"Sentimental Journey" had been playing for a long time, and the trio realized they had been sleeping and that evening shadows were falling across the lake. Up on the trail, a car engine sounded and the ranger pulled into the parking area. He signaled them to come out. they packed up the picnic basket and phonograph and put the empty coke bottles in the sack with the corn whiskey.

The ranger eyed them suspiciously as they pulled even with his vehicle. "You haven't broken any of the rules, have you?" he asked anxiously.

"Not any that I can think of," Spencer said.

"But he can't think too straight right now," Mikey offered, and Darnelle shrieked with laughter. The ranger was not amused.

"I'll need to know your names," he said.

"Well, I'm Spencer Vinings Tolliver, Jr. This is my brother Michael, and this young lady is Darnelle, and she's a friend."

The ranger only heard the name, Tolliver, and he was instantly apologetic for having questioned them. He offered to keep the park open a little longer if they wished him to do so.

"No, my good man. Take the rest of the day off!" Michael said, as he collapsed into the back seat. It had been a day to remember, and it was only when Darnelle saw Mattie's worried expression that she felt some remorse for the length of it.

The strong, sweet smell of the whiskey was quite noticeable to Mattie Lou Herndon. She immediately took Darnelle by the arm and informed the boys there would be no more outings if they were to be mixed with Pike's alcohol.

All three swore that they wouldn't dare drink again if Mattie would relent and allow Darnelle to join them again at the park.

Chapter 12

"Lost Weekend," with Ray Milland, was playing at the Mulberry Theatre, and Michael wanted very much to see it. Spencer was going off for the evening with some fraternity brothers who were picking him up on the way to Atlanta; therefore, the convertible would be left in the driveway. Michael wanted to see the movie, but he wanted to see it with Darnelle. He didn't believe there would be any difficulty with the management because Darnelle had long brown hair, very light coloring, and her eyes were a bluish sort of green, like the color of the water in the pool at the granite quarry in Lithonia.

He didn't want to debate the matter with Spencer, so he just asked to borrow Spencer's convertible to take Darnelle for a drive. Spencer gave his consent but warned Michael to remember not to grind the gears, and to put the top up if it looked like rain. Michael asked Spencer if he took him to be an idiot, and Spencer laughed, stating that that was an affirmative. The deal was made, and Mattie said Darnelle could go provided no drinking was involved.

Michael wanted to take Darnelle to the picture show, but he wanted very much to have some time with her before the movie started, so he headed the car down the road toward the Bogart State Park.

"It'll be dark soon, but we've got a little time before the show starts," he said. "Could we just drive around a bit?"

"Why not? I love riding in this convertible. It makes you feel so...in tune with your surroundings," she said.

"I think you are always in tune," Michael said.

"How sweet of you, Michael. Are you always so gallant with the ladies in Athens?"

Michael shook his head. "There are ladies in Athens, but I don't really care about meeting anyone there."

"Aw, come on Mikey, you know you have a love interest somewhere that you're not telling me about." Michael drove in silence for several minutes. Darnelle sensed that he was upset and put her hand on his arm. "Don't mind me, Mikey," she said. "I was just kidding around. You don't have to tell me anything you don't want to."

Michael started to answer but noticed a car pulling close behind them and directed his attention to the rear view mirror. The car had two black men in the front seat. It was a long red Hudson, and they were now uncomfortably close.

"Hey," Michael said, "What do you think is wrong with those guys behind us?" Darnelle turned to look and gasped as the driver made an obscene gesture in her direction. "Let's turn around, Mikey," she said, and her voice was strained and frightened.

"Why? Who are those guys anyway?"

"One of them is a man called Birdie Lee. I met him at Mrs. Jacobs' the other day, and he's not very nice."

"Well, he can go to hell," Michael said.

Darnelle was insistent now. "Please Mikey, I want to go home. I'm afraid of him."

Michael could feel alarm in his own voice as he tried to reassure her. "We'll turn around at the next crossing," he said.

The red car behind them got even closer, then bumped them from the rear. Michael was really angry now because it was Spencer's car, and he didn't want anything to happen to it.

"Get the hell away from us!" he yelled back over his shoulder.

The men in the Hudson laughed and bumped them again. Michael braked the car and pulled over to the side of the road.

"No, Mikey! Don't stop here! Keep going, keep going!"

The men in the red car pulled alongside of them. Birdie Lee leaned across Sly Joe and smirked at the young couple.

"You giving it away to the white boy?" he asked.

"Shut your filthy mouth!" Michael shouted.

"Hey, listen to the white boy," Birdie said. "I wonder if he can back up his big mouth?"

"One way to find out," Sly Joe answered, as he opened the passenger door of the Hudson, climbed out and moved to Michael's side of the convertible.

Birdie Lee got out from the driver's side of his car. He came around to the passenger's side of Spencer's car and leaned over Darnelle. She moved closer to Michael.

"Just leave us alone," she whimpered. Terror in her voice was evident.

"Aw now, honey," Birdie said. "We won't hurt you none…you don't belong with this white boy. We can show you a lot more fun!"

"Yeah," Sly Joe said. "This little gal way too good fo dis white boy." He reached across Michael and grabbed at Darnelle's breast.

Michael suddenly ground the gears. The car leapt forward leaving Sly Joe reeling from the impact. Now, the chase was on in earnest. Michael literally flew down the graveled road, the car becoming airborne at the crest of the next hill. When the wheels hit the ground again, it jerked the steering from his grasp, causing him to lose control of the car. The convertible sailed across the road, down a steep incline, through a barbed wire fence. The right wheel hit a big boulder. The car careened on its side and slid for twenty yards on the soft pasture grass.

Darnelle lay on top of Michael. When he looked at her, he was afraid she wasn't breathing. He made an effort to slide out onto the grass, thankful the car hadn't flipped upside down and crushed them. He lifted Darnelle gently off his chest and reached backward, feeling a sharp rock behind him. He shifted around it and out of the car.

He heard them coming, heard them laughing, and an insane fury gripped him. He felt for the rock, gripped it in his right hand, and hurtled himself upward and in the direction of the voices.

"Heah come de white dude," Sly Joe said.

Michael lunged and hit Sly Joe with the rock. Immediately, the switchblade came out of Sly Joe's pocket like a reflex, and he caught Michael under the arm, slashing downward across his ribs. Michael felt like a hot poker had burned him.

Headlights stabbed the twilight up on the road, and Sly Joe grabbed Birdie Lee by the arm. "Let's git outa heah," he said. The men ran up the incline, climbed in the Hudson, and roared away just as a farmer's pickup reached the scene.

"Anybody hurt down there?" he called.

"Yes!" The voice came from Darnelle. For a moment Michael forgot the pain in his side and the blood on his shirt. The farmer insisted on taking them to the doctor's house to get the slash wound treated.

"How'd you do this?" The doctor looked keenly at Michael.

"I…I wrecked my car…my brother's car. Must have cut it on some broken glass."

"Looks like a knife wound to me," the doctor said.

"No, it had to have been glass," Michael said.

They left the doctor's office, Michael feeling pleased that he had been able to endure the stitching without showing how much it hurt.

"We'll get a taxi home," he told the farmer, "but I'd like to pay you for your trouble."

The farmer was offended. "If you can't help a accident victim without getting paid, you ain't much account."

"Well, we thank you," Darnelle said.

"You just don't know how much," Michael added, as the farmer cranked his pickup and drove away.

"We have to tell Mama what happened," Darnelle said.

"I'm afraid so," Michael agreed, "But the really rough part is telling Spencer about his car."

"He'll not be mad at you," Darnelle said. "You were absolutely the bravest man I've ever seen."

Michael looked out the window of the cab, and he suddenly found the courage to say what he had planned to say before all of the bad stuff ruined their evening.

"I don't know any other way to do this," he said. "It's just that…that I can't go on pretending any longer that we're kids again. Things have changed, you know. We're not kids; we're practically grownups. People have gotten married at our age."

"What are you trying to say, Mickey?" Darnelle asked, but she was pretty sure that she knew the answer.

"I love you," Michael blurted. "I…I want to marry you."

"I love you too," Darnelle whispered, "but not that way Mickey. We can't love each other that way."

"Why not?" Michael's voice was as wounded as his side. "You don't love me, do you?"

"Yes, I love you. I'll always love you."

"Then why…why for God's sake?"

"Because… I'm your sister," she said.

"No! No…" Mikey's voice came in an agonized whisper. "Oh my God no…you have to be mistaken."

"No mistake, Mikey. There's absolutely no mistake. The judge is my father, too."

Michael sat as if turned to stone. Darnelle reached for him and cradled his head in her arms.

Michael Tolliver had never known his mother. He had only known a man who called himself his father. There had never been a close bond between them, but now Michael hated Judge Spencer Tolliver more than any man on earth.

Michael and Darnelle didn't spare any of the details about the encounter with Birdie Lee Johnson and Sly Joe Willis. After listening to their story, Mattie was so troubled by it she couldn't sleep that night. The judge would be coming home. He might find out about the two of them and her complicity in their dangerous encounter. How could they explain the wrecked car…the slash wound in Michael's side? How could they explain such a thing? She had not a clue, but she feared the judge's wrath more than anything—and she tried to cover it up, tried to make it go away.

She sent Darnelle back to Tuskegee and suggested the boys go back to Athens and await developments. She had a sick feeling about the outcome.

Chapter 13

Old Doc Blanchard saw his last patient before the lunch hour and went into his private bathroom next to his office. He combed his hair in the mirror over the washbasin and stuck his tongue out. He frowned and examined the white patches that had been developing on the sides of his tongue.

"Goddamn cigarettes," he muttered as he removed the half pack from his shirt pocket, crumpled it, and threw it in the waste can. He carefully washed his hands in the sink and dried them on the fresh towel the nurse had put up for him.

The lunch counter was downstairs underneath his office in Turner's Drug Store. He had an outside staircase for patients to enter his waiting room and an inside back staircase for his private entrance and exit. He liked the inside staircase because he could steal a few minutes away from the bellyaches and bunions and smoke a cigarette or two with nobody watching him.

Turner's Drugs was the lunchtime meeting place for the locals. The lunch counter was as good as could be found for Brunswick stew and chili. The BLT's and cheeseburgers were a heavy favorite also. Melvin Turner looked up from the pharmacy counter and nodded as the doctor went by.

"Bowl a chili, cup a coffee, and a grilled cheese," the doctor yelled over the clatter of dishes and loud voices. He took a stool at the counter and swiveled around to nod at the State Farm insurance man and the used car dealer. The grill man stood there grinning and made no effort to fill the order.

"You don't want a cheeseburger?" the grill man asked.

"You running a special?" the doc asked.

"Yeah...two extra spoons a grease per burger."

"Sounds like a deal," the doc said, "but I'll stick to the grilled cheese."

Judge Spencer Tolliver came into the drugstore from the front door. The lady by the register greeted him, and the other patrons looked up and spoke to the judge. He nodded, smiled, and took one of the wire-framed chairs, moving it to the table by the State Farm man.

The State Farm man nodded, then grinned at the doctor and indicated an empty chair at the next table. "Wanna get off that stool and join the brain trust over here?"

The doctor ignored the question and grumbled to the grill man. "Do you know the man who just spoke to me?"

"Never saw him before," the grill man said.

"I don't eat chili with strangers," the doc told the insurance man.

"Have it your own way, Doc. But by the way, we just got notice of a premium increase."

"Send the damn food over to his table," the doc muttered, and he got up and took a seat next to the used car dealer. The used car dealer had once sold new Chevrolets, but the war years had pretty much eliminated that business and put him into the more realistic and more profitable business of dealing in used cars.

The car dealer was the one who spilled the beans.

"Sure hated to see that little convertible of Spencer Junior's get towed last week," the dealer said.

"I haven't heard about it," the judge said. "I just got back from Washington though and the boys had gone back to school." He suddenly frowned. "Do you mean the car has a problem?"

The dealer chuckled. "Yessir, I'd say it had quite a problem. The frame's bent, the radiator's stove in, and the whole left side of it looks like it shared the road with a Sherman tank."

The judge paled under his summer tan, and his hands tapped nervously on the tabletop. "My boy's not hurt is he?"

The dealer cleared his throat and shook his head. "Jeez, I didn't know you hadn't heard about it," he said, "but I don't reckon anybody was hurt. Leastwise, I haven't heard anything...have y'all?"

There was an awkward silence around the table. The doctor coughed and called the counterman, "Bring some more ketchup for the chili...got to dilute this slop."

"Well, hey, I gotta get back to the office," the State Farm man said.

"Hey, me too," the car dealer said, leaving the judge and doctor at the table.

"Well," the doctor said, "there might be something you need to know about."

The judge listened with growing concern as the doctor told him about the night visit to his home and the slash wound that did not look like something gotten in the wreck but more like the work of a knife blade.

"And something else," the doctor said, "Your boy Michael had a girlfriend with him. They seemed to be pretty close, just from my observation."

"A fairly normal situation for a boy his age, I should think." the judge said.

"Well, she was a looker, no question on that...but she was just a little off color, if you know what I mean."

"I sure as hell don't," the judge said, and he pushed his chair back from the table and left like he was going to a fire.

The doctor shook his head and walked back to the pharmacy. "The shit just hit the fan," he told the druggist, "and by God, gimme a pack a Luckies and don't say one damn word." He grabbed the pack and clumped noisily up the stairs.

"I want to know something, Mattie," the judge said, his voice taking on that carefully enunciated form that warned her of the perilous charge of emotion behind it. She stood silently in the kitchen, her throat so tight she could hardly breathe.

"I want to know why you didn't mention one word to me about a car wreck or about my son being injured. I want to know why both my boys are back in Athens and why Darnelle took herself away so fast to Tuskegee after all your lobbying for her visit. I want to know these things right now.

Mattie started wringing her hands, and the judge walked quickly toward her and slapped her face with his open palm. Mattie cowered against the wall.

"You tell me right now," he said.

"They...she...uh..."

"Out with it woman!" the judge demanded as he held his arm upright with the palm open, Mattie cringing against the kitchen wall.

"They were in a wreck," she finally said.

"I know damn well there was a wreck," the judge said. "What I don't know is why Darnelle and Michael were in Spencer's car in the first place. What is the answer to that?"

"He...he...Mikey... wanted to take her for a ride, just for a ride..."

"You knew better than to allow that," the judge said.

Mattie nodded and went on. "I did know better. I just didn't see..."

"What happened next, Mattie? What caused the wreck?"

And she had to tell it all.

Chapter 14

Judge Spencer Vinings Tolliver sat behind his big mahogany desk and made a steeple of his fingertips. The fingers were long and slender, and they did not tremble nor did they show any sign of the rage that boiled inside the man.

A totally unacceptable condition had occurred in his realm. Not only had the life of his son been threatened, but also the daughter he had never acknowledged in public had suffered the attentions of an ignorant, worthless troublemaker, intent on raping her. The fact that the man was a Negro made the gorge rise in his throat.

"This is how we're going to handle this thing," the judge said.

Sheriff Lee Junkins and the two deputies stood just inside the door of Judge Tolliver's study, the door tightly closed.

"Nobody breathes a word about this incident outside this room. There will be no public hearing and no arrest warrants issued. We know the guilty party, and we know his accomplice, so there is no real need for the public expense of bringing them to justice."

The sheriff shuffled his feet uneasily. "Well, I guess the KKK would think the same way...but I'm supposed to uphold the law..."

Judge Tolliver raised his arm for silence, his face hard with anger, and his blue-green eyes boring into the sheriff.

"You are expected to do as you are told," he said. "I AM the law in Mulberry. I am the one who decides how punishment is administered." He looked at the two deputies. "How would you like to work for Mutt Shelton?"

The deputies laughed at the joke, but the judge wasn't joking. The sheriff looked as if he was stricken with a cramp.

"What I'm saying here," the judge explained, "is that I can hang that sheriff's badge on someone as dumb as Mutt Shelton or as smart as my Blue Tick Hound. I decide the vote in Bogart County. You know that as well as anybody, sheriff. It has worked to your advantage for these many years; so don't get yourself confused about your job. Just do as you're told."

The sheriff nodded dolefully and looked at the floor.

"We are going to remove the perpetrators from Bogart County," the judge said, "by whatever means are necessary. It is a fact of life that a crime has been committed here. It is a fact of life that we have a niggra agitator here, and it is a fact of life that the peace and tranquility of our place of residence has been repeatedly disturbed."

He looked directly at the sheriff once more. "You don't have to be involved in the removal process," he said. "In fact, I feel it would be best if you and your two deputies here found a reason to be in another part of the county tomorrow. Is that understood?"

The sheriff nodded vigorously, relieved to be absolved of responsibility. The deputies also seemed relieved. "But do remember," the judge said, "where your paycheck originates, and think about what you would do without Fanny's protection money."

"I don't know…" the sheriff blustered.

"Yes, you do," the judge said. "You know perfectly well what I'm talking about. I could make one telephone call and have all three of you doing time at Reidsville. Do I make myself clear?"

The sheriff nodded; the deputies nodded, and the judge seemed satisfied. "You deputies can go on home now, the judge said. "The sheriff and I have some other things to discuss."

The other thing was not exactly a discussion. The judge laid it out in no uncertain terms. There was still a job for the sheriff that the deputies didn't need to know about in the successful removal of the perpetrators.

The sheriff's job was surveillance. There was a need to keep track of the perpetrators, and there was no doubt that Fanny's place should be kept under observation. A phone call had to be made to the mill office at the exact time the perpetrators left Fanny's parking lot.

His meeting with the shift supervisor at the Mulberry Cotton Mill lasted much longer.

The supervisor was Joe Bradley, who had literally grown up in the cotton mill, earning his position by dent of hard work and loyalty to Judge Tolliver. Their planning had to include different scenarios. There was the real possibility of endangerment to the mill workers involved, and, of course, this risk had to be minimized. They had to be certain that the perpetrator's car was stopped, and one way to do that was to put a rifle slug through one of the front ties. Joe Bradley would handle that job and direct the action to follow.

"Are you familiar with the term 'justifiable homicide'? the judge asked, and Joe Bradley nodded.

"I guess it means it's all right to kill somebody," he said.

"Not in that general sense," the judge answered, "but when there are extenuating circumstances…I mean when your life is threatened or the lives of your family are threatened…when someone breaks into your home or into your automobile and seeks to do bodily harm, then, under those circumstances, well yes, one might consider that a justifiable condition."

Joe Bradley nodded, and the judge looked at him. Joe shifted his feet.

"In my years on the bench," the judge said, "I've even known cases where a child might actually KILL A PARENT when the child's life or the lives of siblings might be subjected to repeated abuse."

The judge pursed his lips and looked thoughtfully at Joe Bradley. "We would, of course, need to know the case in order to make the right judicial decision."

Joe Bradley's face paled for a moment, and he wondered just how much the judge knew about his childhood upbringing. He shifted his feet again and stared out the window.

The judge swiveled the chair around. Now his eyes bored into Joe in a way that made him feel like a bird roasting on a spit. "We don't want those people in our county," he said, and Joe nodded. "We also don't want them to LEAVE this county. This is one of those times when we have to look at what is justifiable. Do you understand me, Joe Bradley?"

"Yessir," Joe said, "I understand you want them to be dead."

The judge nodded.

Joe Bradley picked his men carefully. There were 20 men from the second shift. They were off duty, and they were loyal workers. They were told that their job was to "scare the shit out of some uppity niggers," and they would need guns for protection in case the niggers resisted in any way. He told the men the niggers were armed and dangerous and that they had already wounded a white man, so they should not take any chances.

Mutt Shelton said he was going to bring a Thompson submachine gun. The other men laughed at the idea, but he was adamant. He said it had belonged to his daddy, a model 1921 and would fire .45 caliber bullets at the rate of 800 rounds per minute.

Chapter 15

"We got a problem, judge." The voice on the telephone belonged to Sheriff Junkins.

The judge swiveled his chair away from the desk in the courthouse office, stood up, and walked to the door of the office, closing it.

"What problems do I need to hear about in this office?" he asked into the phone.

"Well, it's more people than we expected."

"Listen carefully now. You are the sheriff of this county, and you have a job to do. Any problems you have, or think you might have, you discuss those with Joe Bradley."

"But Judge…there's four of them in that car…"

"I have no idea what you're talking about, Sheriff. Like I said, you discuss anything that's bothering you with Joe Bradley."

"Yessir, Judge…I just thought…"

"Don't think," the judge said.

Chapter 16

Birdie Lee and Sly Joe spent the early part of the morning in the upstairs bedrooms over the Blue Goose juke joint. The two women worked for the establishment. Fanny Mae furnished them bed and board and took fifty percent of the fees.

Afterward, they came downstairs and ate breakfast, then decided to have a picnic.

"You gals spending the day with us," Birdie Lee said.

"Nah…it's yo ass gone do the spending," the girl named Buttercup laughed.

"What I said is, we spendin' the day down at that Bogart State Park."

"Hey now," Sly Joe said. "You trying' to get in jail again? You know ain't no niggers welcome in that state park."

"I 'bout had me enough a that shit," Birdie replied. "Ain't no sign says we can't go to the damn state park."

"Well, there was a sign at the Mulberry Theatre," Sly Joe said. "It said, 'Colored Upstairs,' and you didn't pay no mind to it, and look what it got us."

"That's just what I'm saying. Ain't no sign at that park."

Sly Joe shook his head. Buttercup went over and put an arm around his shoulders. "You ain't no limp Willie, are you Sly Joe?"

He shoved her arm away and poured a good slug of shine into his coffee cup.

"Gittin' a little liquid courage, Willie Boy?"

Sly Joe set the cup on the table and reached for Buttercup. "Let's go back upstairs."

"Ain't got time for that," Birdie Lee stated. "We got places to go and peoples to see, but first I got to take a pee."

The girls laughed, and Sly Joe took another swig from the coffee cup. Fanny Mae came over and collected in advance for the day.

A short time later the two women and the two men packed a picnic box consisting of two bottles of moonshine, a box of crackers, sardines and cheese, and a carton of Coca-Cola. They loaded it into the red Hudson and pulled out of the parking space onto the road toward the Appalachee Bridge.

Chapter 17

Billy James Bradley came to visit his Uncle Joe Bradley in Mulberry, Georgia, in the early summer of 1945. He had never visited his father's oldest brother before that time.

The reason he came was because his father, Jackson Bradley, had fallen off a barge in the Savannah River in the spring of that year and drowned before he could be rescued. His widow was left with two little girls younger than Billy James, and she had to go to work. Her mother agreed to keep the girls during the workday, but Billy James was 10 years old and too much of a boy for the grandmother.

Joe Bradley invited Billy James to come to Mulberry for the summer. Billy's mother thought it would be good for him to be in the country, so he rode the train to Social Circle; his uncle met him at the station, and they drove on up to Joe Bradley's farm, which was owned by Judge Tolliver.

Joe Bradley was a supervisor at the Mulberry Cotton Mill, and because he was a supervisor, he had a bigger house and more acreage than any of the other employees. He had these perquisites, but he understood, as did all the others, that he, too, was owned by Judge Tolliver.

These conditions did not affect the visit, and, indeed, Billy James was not aware that the conditions existed. He was greatly excited over the opportunity to live outside the big city. He had his own sleeping loft in the uncle's house, and in the nighttime he very often heard the sound of bobcats and owls, and he would be glad he was safely ensconced in the attic.

Billy James had his own morning chores that Aunt Nettie assigned to him. Aunt Nettie did not work at the mill although she had no children to care for during the day. She was a supervisor's wife, and the mill community respected her for that.

Billy James would cut stove wood for the cook stove in the kitchen, and he helped Aunt Nettie hang the sheets on the clothesline in back of the house on washdays. He had lots of free time to play with the Bradley's dog; the dog was enjoying the summer too. He had needed a young boy to throw sticks and rocks and yell for him, and Billy James just fit the bill. Therefore, the dog was always waiting by the door when Billy emerged, and his tail wagged like it was motorized the minute Billy stepped outside.

The only thing that kept the dog from being the ideal companion was the fact he couldn't converse with Billy; he just barked, and often at the wrong time or the wrong place. Billy James began to talk for the dog, and this worked out very well. "Let's go a little further," he would say for the dog, and then he would answer, "Okay, let's do that." After a time, he didn't notice that he was talking for the dog, it just seemed like the dog had a mind of his own, and could speak to him, or argue with him, or bring up any point of conversation.

Neither Aunt Nettie nor Billy James knew about the trouble that was brewing in the town on the day she sent him out to pick blackberries. Nobody knew outside Uncle Joe Bradley and the men at the mill, and the sheriff's department, and of course, Judge Spencer Tolliver.

Billy and the mixed breed dog, whose name was Lectric and had gotten the name because of his motorized tail, had reached the fencerow below the bridge that crossed the Appalachee River. They had gone much further than Aunt Nettie would have approved, but when he spotted lush, ripe berries further along the fence, he couldn't very well just walk away.

When they heard the first sounds of the engines coming around the curve above the bridge, they crouched back under the vines and waited to see who was coming. Lectric would likely have boldly investigated the noise, but Billy would have no part of it. For a ten-year-old boy, there is a need for tunnels and caves, and secret places under vines and such. The boy and the dog began to talk about the engines as they waited in the hollowed out spot under the vines where some deer or hog or some other wild beast had rested.

The engine sounds got closer. Then, the first vehicle came around the curve and pulled over in the grass beside the road. A man got out of the car and began signaling each vehicle, one on the left side of the road and the other to the right, back and forth, so that both sides of the road had vehicles parked, three on each side of the road. There were two flatbed trucks with big dual wheels on the rear and four pickup trucks. Some were Fords and Chevrolets and Billy James could see the flatbeds were Dodge trucks.

The flatbeds had men sitting on them. Billy James could recognize two of them. One was Mr. Jack Riggins, and the other was Mr. Eulie Benson. They both worked for his Uncle Joe at the cotton mill. Billy saw that they had rifles across their laps, but, on further observation, Billy noticed that all the men had guns.

"I see Uncle Joe," Billy said.

"I see him too," Billy spoke for the dog.

"He's got a gun, looks like a rifle."

"Why do they have all those guns?" Billy asked for the dog.

"I bet I know," Billy whispered. There's been a jailbreak for sure, and they're going to catch the convicts."

"How do you know?"

"Cause I saw convicts working on the road last week. They was all chained together, and they was slinging blades to cut the grass."

"Hey, what if the convicts is hiding in these blackberry bushes right behind us?" Billy asked for the dog.

"They might be hidin' and then again, they might have stolen a car and are coming toward the bridge from back yonder."

The men from the cars and trucks started loading the guns, then, they started looking down the road where Billy and Lectric were hiding in the vines. One of them had a funny looking gun with a round sort of can in front of the handle.

"I think something bad is going to happen," Billy said. He could feel an anxiety building within himself.

"I want to go back home Billy," he spoke for the dog.

"Well, okay, but we got to be quiet. If they see the bushes moving, they might shoot at us instead of the convicts."

There was a car engine sound now. It was down the road behind them. Suddenly a long, red passenger car came into view, coming pretty fast, judging by the dust cloud boiling up behind it. The car got even with their hiding place, and Billy James could see it was a Hudson with a Negro man and woman in the front seat, and another Negro couple in the rear. They were laughing, and one of the men threw a glass bottle out of the window. It hit a big rock on the opposite side of the road, and pieces of glass flew up in the air. The people in the car laughed some more.

They were past where Billy James and Lectric were hiding and almost to the bridge when a rifle shot rang out. Something happened to the wheel on the car, and the driver was jerking at the steering to hold it on the road. The car spun around in the gravel. It made two big circles and almost went off the edge of the road before it stopped.

Billy James had a hard job holding Lectric down under the vines, but he could see the people in the car and they weren't laughing any more.

Both of the men got out of the car to look at the blown out tire. A moment later, the colored men looked up and across the bridge and saw all the white men with guns. One black man yelled, "Don't shoot, we ain't done nuthin!"

Birdie Lee reached back inside the car. Billy James thought he was helping the woman out of the car, but then he saw the colored man had a gun, too. It looked like a pistol with a long barrel or a rifle with a short barrel. Peering harder, Billy James saw that it was neither; it was just a lug wrench the Negro man was holding out in front of him.

Then, everything got all blurry with explosions and screaming. The colored man with the lug wrench fell beside the car, and the other colored man came running in their direction. The women were stretched out head to head with their arms extended like they were trying to reach out to someone.

There was a different sound now, and the explosions came all together, so fast you couldn't count them. Billy heard the branches of the trees cracking above his head, and he felt something pretty big hit just above his head. He laid low and pushed Lectric down in the grass and dirt under the blackberry vines. Then, the vines shook above them like a covey of quail had been flushed out of the branches.

Everything got awful quiet—not the sound of a bird or anything at all. Billy James raised his head just a little and looked through a hole in the vines. The other colored man was lying in the road just ten feet away. Billy James could see his face was torn; blood was running from his mouth and into the dirt.

There were other holes in the man's clothes, and Billy James could see dark stains from where the blood was running into the gravel. The man's feet were still digging at the dirt, then suddenly they stopped. Billy James felt very sick to his stomach.

Something was dripping down on his neck. He looked up and saw some gray matter, then, the outline of a lower jaw. The jaw had a gold tooth, and it was sparkling in the ray of sunlight at the top of the vines. Blood was dripping from the severed piece of jaw, and Billy saw that his own shirt collar was wet from the blood that was dripping down on him.

He began to scream then, a high-pitched, wailing scream that went on without end, and the dog began to howl as well. In a flash, he and the dog were running through the brambles and vines toward the roadway and the bridge.

"What the hell?" a voice called.

"Put down that gun, you damned fool! It's some kid. By God, I said to put down the gun!" another said.

There was a frantic shuffling of feet across the bridge, and Billy James ran as hard as he could, but the men caught him before he reached the end of the fence. Billy's heart was pounding.

"It's Joe Bradley's kid," one of the men whispered.

"Nah, it's Joe Bradley's nephew," Mr. Jack Riggins said.

But, they couldn't stop the screaming, and they waited for Joe Bradley to come. When he caught up to them, he stuck out his arm and slapped Billy James full in the face. Billy fell to the ground, and he stopped screaming.

Chapter 18

The judge, frowning from his position behind the great mahogany desk in his study that he had inherited from his father said, "Well, it would appear that we have some loose ends here. Loose ends can be a problem…in a cotton mill…or in a delicate situation like this."

Joe Bradley took on a look of acute anxiety. He had spent all of his adult life working in the judge's employ. He had finally gotten the manager's job, and he could feel all of it somehow hinging on this conversation in the judge's office.

"It looks as if your nephew…you say his name is Billy James? Yes, well, it appears that Billy James was in the wrong place at the wrong time."

"I can handle my nephew," Joe Bradley said quickly, looking for some way to tie up the loose ends the judge had mentioned.

The judge nodded thoughtfully and made a steeple of his fingertips. "Oftentimes," the judge said, "we have the impression that we can handle people, and it turns out that we cannot. People are different, you see, and some are motivated in a manner that we understand…and then others…well, you see what I mean."

"Yessir," Joe Bradley said, but he didn't see at all what the judge was talking about. He just felt that his butt was in a sling because his nephew had witnessed the killings. It shouldn't have happened, and somehow he knew he was responsible.

"I can handle my nephew," he said again.

The judge looked at him with those blue-green eyes that seemed to bore right into his soul. "Does your nephew love you?" he asked.

Joe Bradley was confused. It seemed the question was not relevant to the matter at hand, but he had to answer. "Yessir," he said. "I suppose that he does. He ain't had no call to not love me I reckon."

"Does he love your wife, Nettie?"

"Well, yessir, I suppose he loves her too. He ain't had…"

The judge raised his hand and Joe Bradley stopped speaking. "These are very important questions," the judge said solemnly. "They have to do with family ties, you see. Family ties are something we have come to count on. They matter most when the chips are down."

"I suppose so," Joe Bradley answered, but the judge shook his head.

"We can't suppose, Joe Bradley. We have to be certain. If family ties are important to young Billy James, then he will keep his mouth shut and go back home to Augusta."

"He loves us," Joe Bradley said meekly, miserably, but immeasurably relieved to hear a solution short of executing the child.

"You understand he must go back home to Augusta. That is in the best interests of everybody…" The judge drew that word out in slow measure. "Best for everybody…if he doesn't come back here." He stood up then, walked around the desk and placed an arm on Joe Bradley's shoulder. "He can never come back here, not ever."

"I understand," Joe Bradley said. Then, he spoke about what had troubled him almost as much as his nephew. "We have a problem, Judge. It's Otis Caswell. He came into the mill office this morning and told me he had stayed awake all night long and said he had been thinking about it, and he had decided to confess his part in it. Said he was going to tell the preacher, and they were going to talk to God about it."

"Then we must help him," the judge said.

His name was Otis Caswell, and he was pale and visibly frightened when he was called up to the mill manager's office. He looked surprised to see the sheriff sitting there. He looked at Joe Bradley, and Joe shook his head. "What's going on?" Otis asked.

"You better come along now," the sheriff said.

"But…"

"No buts…stick your arms out here." The sheriff put the cuffs on Otis and shoved him along in front of him toward the door. Otis looked back over his shoulder. Joe Bradley just nodded at him. The sheriff pushed him out the door and down the steps to his car. He opened the back door of the car, put his hand on Otis' head and pushed him down in the seat.

The sheriff drove out of the mill parking lot and headed out on the county road toward the park. "Where're we going?" Otis asked.

"Shut your mouth," the sheriff said.

He drove along for some time. Otis kept his mouth shut and looked out the window at the heat waves shimmering over the cotton fields.

The sheriff turned down a dirt side road that led to Big Moccasin Creek. The dust flew up all around them, and Otis couldn't see much, but he knew it was the wrong direction. The sheriff parked the car in the turnaround by the creek, got out of the car, and walked around the area like he was looking for something or somebody, but then, he seemed satisfied about it and came back to the car.

"Come out of there," he said.

Otis turned afraid and pushed himself into a corner of the back seat as far from the sheriff as possible.

"Listen, Sheriff," he said, "I was going to confess…"

"Shut your mouth," the sheriff said, and he reached in and grabbed Otis by the belt buckle, and yanked him out of the car. Otis fell face down in the soft dirt. The sheriff took his big flashlight and hit Otis in the back of his head. It made a crunching sound, and Otis went limp.

The sheriff looked all around again. When he didn't see or hear anybody, he walked back to where Otis was sprawled in the dirt. He took the handcuffs off, dragged Otis by the heels to the edge of the creek, and pushed him over into the water. He got a big rock and placed it by Otis's head. The water ran on top of the rock, over Otis's face, making little gurgling sounds over the new barrier toward its progress down stream.

The sheriff broke a branch off a small pine and swept the area clean. Then, he put the branch in the back seat of the car so he could throw it out at a different place. He opened the glove compartment of the car and took out the bulky, manila envelope the judge had given him. He looked inside the flap and saw bills all of one hundred-dollar denomination.

The sheriff began to feel better.

Chapter 19

The Spring Branch Holy Ghost Church was filled to capacity with a substantial spillover crowd milling in and around the parking area. Because it was hot, all the windows were open and wasps circled in and out of the windows, disturbed by the people's presence and the possible threat to the nests in the corners of the building.

Dirt daubers, too, showed concern, but were not as militant in their over flight. The dirt daubers had stippled the narrow ceiling planks with row upon row of red mud habitats, many of which had dried out during the hot summer and crumbled off, onto the floors and hard backed benches.

Nobody noticed the insects because all eyes were upon the four silver caskets resting on a sawhorse platform in front of the altar. The platform was covered with flowers, most of them home grown and picked on the way to the funeral service. There was only an occasional murmur of noise from the children, which was promptly hushed by the adults. The atmosphere in and around the church was charged with a tension not normal to a church gathering or a funeral.

Birdie Lee Johnson's mother did not attend the services. She was certain that the white killers would execute her in the same manner as her son, and so she stayed inside her house with the shades drawn and the windows closed and endured the stifling heat of the day.

The Reverend Willie James Wilcox presided for the opening prayers and supplications, but Bishop Eugene D. Stringfellow, graduate of Morehouse College in Atlanta and presiding Bishop of the Holy Ghost Church in Forest Park, Georgia, preached the funeral sermon. The bishop, slight of stature, stood. He was dressed in black, the only contrast being his white clerical collar and a single rose in his lapel. His face showed no emotion, but the eyes were alive, and the audience settled and waited for him to begin.

"We will take our text from The First Epistle of John," the preacher said. Although he didn't say it loudly, his voice was heard all the way to the back row. "Chapter Three and verse fifteen...Whosoever hateth his brother is a murderer...and ye know that no murderer hath eternal life abiding in him. Let the audience say amen." Faint murmurs and whispers of amen throughout the church and muffled sobs came from the relatives of the victims. "And in chapter four, verse twenty...If a man say, 'I love God,' and hateth his brother, he is a liar."

Bishop Stringfellow closed *TheBible* and laid it on the pulpit. He closed his eyes for just a moment, then, looked from one face to another. "You have heard it straight from the holy book...a man who claims to love God, and at the same time, hates his brother is a liar and a murderer."

"Yes, Lord."

"There are men somewhere in this county today who are guilty of hatred. There are men sitting in their own houses of worship today claiming to love God, and they are liars, according to the holy book...liars and murderers before God, and no murderer has eternal life abiding in him."

"Have mercy, Lord!"

"A wind of CHANGE is coming, brethren...a wind that will lift the murderers up like chaff in a cyclone, and sweep them away. No mortal man can withstand the will of God nor stay the hand of judgment. Vengeance is MINE, sayeth the Lord!"

"Amen and AMEN!"

"I have quoted to you from the holiest of books," the bishop said, "and I will quote to you from one of our own, the great Booker T. Washington, who said, 'I shall never permit myself to stoop so low as to hate ANY man.' Let the people say amen."

The response was greater now, confidence building in the words of the preacher. "Say on, brother," and "Yes, Lord God Almighty," came from the far corners of the building.

"The seeds of hate," the bishop said, "are planted in this Georgia soil, but that wind of change will expose them to the white heat of the day and blow them to the far corners of the universe…to a barren and forbidding landscape that allows no seed to germinate."

"Praise God…let it be, Precious Lord!"

The funeral service lasted for an hour and forty-five minutes. Throughout that time men stood in the doorway and on the sides, and in back of the building. Vigilant men with eyes turned toward the road and toward the woods, ready to sound the alarm, ready with the guns, if need be. Not all of them found comfort in the bishop's proclamations.

"I don't know 'bout dat wind he talking 'bout…maybe HE jes fulla wind fo' all I kin tell."

"Say on, ain't no change coming way out here in Bogart County. Maybe he see somethin' back there in Atlanta, but it ain' presented itself to de peoples out here."

"We gone be lookin' at de same old dirt daubers wen we come back nex' Sunday. Gone be dodgin' dem wasps and dodgin' dem dirt daubers, and at's how it's gone be. Ain' nothing gone change 'roun heah."

But something did change. There weren't any dirt daubers nor any wasps to plague the congregation the next Sunday. There was no church building, either. It burned to the ground in the dark hours after midnight following the funeral.

Chapter 20

"Willie, I don't have any words that are adequate to express my sorrow, I just…"Joe Bryant shook his head and looked at Willie James Wilcox. Willie was seated on the edge of his front porch, his face impassive. His voice came at last, and he nodded toward the screen door behind him. "Don't you think you'd be better off inside, instead of out here in the daylight where prying eyes can see you?"

"I don't care about the prying eyes," Joe Bryant said. "I don't care much about the rest of the anatomy that goes with them either. I have to tell you that I'm leaving this place."

"Nah…you ain't serious about that."

"Yes, I'm afraid I am. I can't get over the feeling there might be murderers and church burners sitting alongside the other churchgoers…singing the same hymns, professing to love God and their fellow man. The idea is repugnant to me."

"What about your call to preach?"

Joe dropped his head. "I can't really tell you if there ever was one. Wasn't ever a blinding flash or a voice from the heavens…my Mama just told me from the time I was in grade school that I was going to be a preacher. Said her brother was a preacher, and she intended me to carry on the family tradition.

Well, I went off to Bible College down in Graceville, Florida, and that's where I was when the call came to go into the service.

They looked at my records and assigned me to the Chaplain's Corps. I stayed there until the war was over, and then I decided to try my hand at a regular church. Needless to say, it hasn't worked out for me."

"Well, Joe, I'd say there's a heap of preachers in the same boat with you, not knowing for sure if they are really called."

"I don't know. I'm sure there are some who are very convinced that God is talking directly to them...that actually hear the voice of God speaking. That's not happening to me."

"You're young Joe...very young...and you got to learn to be patient."

"I find it hard to be patient with a community of people intent on the destruction of a house of God just because colored folks worship there."

"That wasn't none of God's doin, Joe Bryant. That was the Devil himself. The Devil got his messengers too, you know. They be testing the faith of my flock." Willie looked very sad. He got up from the porch and stood in front of Joe Bryant. He placed a hand on Joe Bryant's shoulder. "You ain't going to be able to help yourself or any of us by quitting the preaching profession." he said.

Joe moved back a step and avoided the hand. "Don't try to talk me out of it Willie. I've always felt...well, sometimes I wonder if my God is the same one I read about in the Bible. Seems like the authors put way too many human characteristics on the face of God. Sure...a God of love, a God of compassion, an all seeing, all knowing entity, but then a God also of vengeance, of anger, of capricious selection of his chosen..."

"Whoa now," Willie smiled for the first time. "You forgettin' something. The Lord Jesus Christ changed that entire eye for an eye business. He said if somebody slap you up side the head, then you got to turn the other side, so he can slap you again."

"Well, I'm not Jesus," Joe Bryant said.

"Nah, you ain't, and I ain't smart enough to tell you what to do, but I wish you could see your way clear to staying...at least, until the investigation is completed."

"What makes you think there will be an investigation?" Joe Bryant's face hardened. "Judge Tolliver will handle that the same way he handles everything else around here...and it will be swept right under the rug. Yeah, he's got his spies everywhere, and chances are they are looking at the two of us right now, but I'm not worrying about the consequences anymore. I'm going to look that old buzzard in the face and tell him what he can do with his church property."

"You making a mistake, Joe Bryant," Willie James said.

"I'd be making a bigger mistake to knuckle under to that tyrant. Somebody has to tell him he can't play God any longer."

Joe Bryant put the straw hat back on his head and shook hands with Willie James. Then, he got into the old Model A car and headed back to his rooming house. He had never gotten a chance to bring his fiancé to look at the house the judge had offered. Now, it wouldn't be necessary.

Chapter 21

Joe Bryant parked the Model A at the curb in front of the courthouse. He noted there were still hitching rails for horses there, but he doubted any folks used those anymore. There was a black Packard that he recognized as belonging to the judge, parked in a restricted zone at the side entrance of the courthouse. There was another car with "Sheriff" printed in big letters on the doors, and it had a red bubble light on the top.

Joe Bryant walked up the granite steps to the front entrance and into the darkened interior, which smelled of oiled floors and mothballs. He read the signs on the doors for the sheriff's office, and saw the arrow pointing downstairs to the bathrooms and the jail.

There was a water fountain with a white bowl and a ceramic knurled knob to turn the water on and off. The sign above it read "Whites Only". He went to the end of the hall and noted the Justice of the Peace sign with the smaller gold lettering that read "Judge Spencer Vinings Tolliver" underneath. He knocked at the door.

The outer office appeared to be empty, so he walked on in and stood by the counter that ran the length of the room. There was a waist high swinging door that permitted access to the work desk, but nobody was working there. He saw a small bell on the counter and tapped it lightly.

Judge Spencer Tolliver suddenly appeared at the doorway of the private office behind the counter. "Well, well, the Reverend Joe Bryant! Come in. You can push through the swinging door there. It goes either way."

Joe Bryant shook his head. "I guess I can say what I came to say from right here."

The judge pursed his lips and the eyes studied the preacher thoughtfully. "Well, did you come here to talk about the house I offered you?"

"No, I didn't," Joe Bryant said.

"Well, whatever you came to say, let's get on with it. I'm a little busy for small talk today." The judge was no longer smiling.

"I believe you requested that I clear any change of attitude with you," Joe said.

"Well, in the matter that we discussed...yes. I don't want you to upset the community with ideas that are not in keeping with the local view of things."

"Your local view of things is exactly why I'm here," Joe said. "Your local view that it's all right to murder and burn down church buildings..."

"You hold it right there!" The judge's voice was like a mule whip cutting the air. "Where do you think you get off talking to an officer of the court in this manner?"

"I have no respect for your court, judge."

"Think very, very carefully about what you're saying," Judge Tolliver said quietly. "We do not take insults to the judicial system lightly."

Joe Bryant knew he had stepped over the line, but he had gone this far and there was a need to go the rest of the way. "I just wanted you to be the first to know...that I'm resigning the opportunity to serve as your pastor."

The judge smiled thinly. "All things considered, young man, I would say that you have made an excellent decision."

Joe nodded. "I also wanted you to know that it is my intention to request an outside investigation of the murders and the church burning."

"I see," the judge said, and there was no indication that he had any concern. "You've told no one else about this decision?"

"No, as I said, I thought you should be the first to know."

"You were very right to come to me first, preacher." The judge began to smile again. "Let me give you some good advice, Joe Bryant. Don't talk to anyone else about this...at least not about your intentions...for your own safety, understand?"

"If you think I'm concerned about my safety, then you're right," Joe Bryant said. "Any community that harbors murderers and church burners is capable of killing anybody, I suppose. But look at it this way, I was afraid the first time I hit the beachhead at Omaha. I was afraid the first time I saw the mangled body of a friend who stepped on a land mine. Being afraid is a pretty common condition for me."

He turned and walked toward the door to the hallway, then stopped and faced the judge once again.

"I've been afraid of something or somebody most of my life, in spite of my assurance that God was on my side. I expect some of the Germans thought God was on their side too, but we couldn't let their system go unchallenged. That's why young men went into battle, white and colored, because they believed there was a higher purpose than their personal safety."

He looked the judge squarely in the eyes, and in spite of the chilling effect of that exchange, his words were strong and unwavering. "I can't let your system go unchallenged, judge. I can't let your system get away with crimes this horrendous and just keep my mouth shut."

The judge didn't bat an eyelash, and Joe Bryant went through the door and out to the Model A. He noticed the left front tire looked a little low and decided to drop by the service station on the corner.

"Mornin' preacher," the mechanic said as he came out of the service bay. "Fill 'er up?"

"Yes, do that. Fill it up and check this tire on the front. Seems like it has lost some air since yesterday."

"Hey, I've lost a little air since yesterday myself," the mechanic joked, "but your problem is a nail in the tire." He pointed a finger to the nail head protruding between the treads.

"You've got good eyes," Joe said. "I didn't see that until you pointed it out."

"Course, it could be the tire was in a different position when you was lookin'. It won't take more'n twenty minutes or so to put a patch on the tube."

"Sounds like a good idea to me," Joe said.

Back at the courthouse the judge rang the intercom bell to the sheriff's office.

Chapter 22

"What did the preacher want?" the sheriff asked as he hooked a thumb in the broad leather belt and looked down at the mechanic, Rufus Williams, who was lying on a crawler underneath a pickup truck.

Rufus rolled himself out from under the truck and sat upright on the crawler. He wiped grease from his hands on the legs of his coveralls. "Oh him? He just wanted a tank a gas, and I fixed a flat for him. That old car's got pretty thin tires all around."

"Which tire was it?"

"Which tire? It was the left front. I put a Camel patch on the tube, but it looked like it had been patched several places already."

"Well, there's been a war, you know. Tires been hard to get, even for folks with the money to pay for 'em.

"Least you work for the county," Rufus said. "They got to take care of your tires or let all the criminals get away."

The sheriff laughed and spat tobacco juice into the drain. "You know I ain't gonna let criminals get away from me after you done such a good job grinding my valves."

"You got a good motor in that car...that's for sure."

"Preacher didn't say where he was goin', I guess."

"Nah, he didn't say nuthin' about that. Say, he ain't in no trouble or nuthin'?"

"He's a preacher ain't he? Why would he be in any trouble? I was just askin' is all."

Joe Bryant went to his room, packed his few belongings and took them down to the car. The landlady watched out of her front window and saw the bags. She came out of the house and onto the sidewalk.

"Are you takin' a trip, preacher?"

"Yes, I am, Mrs. Bodine." Joe Bryant reached inside the car and took out a few copies of the National Geographic magazine. "I know you enjoy these," he said, as he handed them to her.

"Oh, my…yes, I do indeed, but what about…"

"I'm leaving, Mrs. Bodine. My rent's paid ahead, and I want you to keep it in lieu of notice."

"But…is something wrong? Did I not…"

"It has absolutely nothing to do with you, Mrs. Bodine. You've been a good landlady, and your cornbread is as good as I've ever tasted, but I've got to be going."

"Oh my. I'm so sorry to hear this, so sorry, indeed. I wish you'd tell me why you decided to go. There might have been something I could do."

"You couldn't really. As I said, it has nothing to do with you."

Joe Bryant got into the Model A and waved a salute to Mrs. Bodine. He turned the old car onto the Athens highway. The sun was hot, and the inside of the car was hotter. He craned his neck and stuck his head out of the window, letting the rush of air pass over his face. He was looking straight ahead, driving quickly along the graveled surface. The Appalachee Bridge was just ahead of him, and he didn't notice the car in his rear view mirror until it was too late

The sheriff's car came alongside and then purposefully struck the preacher's car at an angle to the left front tire, spinning him around and through the guardrail. The Model A went upside down into the river.

The sheriff waited by the bridge until the car was out of sight. He waited some more, but nothing came to the surface. He shook his head and looked up and down the roadway but there was no other car in sight.

"You gotta watch out for them old tires," he said.

Chapter 23

Uncle Joe explained it all to Billy James, told him the way it had to be, and if Aunt Nettie knew anything you sure couldn't tell it by the way she carried on when she learned he was going back to Augusta.

"I just don't understand," she said. "I thought we were having a good time…the way you helped with the chores and ran through the fields and played with the dog…"

"I'm homesick,' Billy James said feebly. Then, he burst into tears and ran out of the kitchen.

"I'll be taking him home," Joe Bradley said.

"Do you want me to go along with you?"

"Not this time, Nettie. I think the boy and I should be alone on this trip. It's the manly thing to do under the circumstances."

"But I don't see what harm it would do…"

"I ain't going to argue with you on this," Joe Bradley said.

The trip to Augusta was made in Joe Bradley's Ford pickup. Billy's old suitcase was in the back with the spare tire, and Lectric's doghouse was back there also.

"I'm giving you the dog," Uncle Joe had said, and it was so unexpected that Billy James didn't know what to say. He just grabbed Lectric around the stomach and hoisted him up in his arms and Lectric's tail went a mile a minute.

Billy hugged Aunt Nettie and told her he had enjoyed his visit, and he was sorry about getting homesick and all. She told him that was all right, and he must come again, but he knew he never would.

"Son," Uncle Joe said, as they rolled down old highway 287 toward Augusta, "there's going to be some questions in your mind about what happened back there, some things that you won't be able to understand at your young age."

"I don't think I'll ever understand it," Billy answered.

"Yes, you will," Uncle Joe said. "When you get to be a man, and you see how hard it is to take on responsibility...when you know that there's a lot of people depending on you to make the right decisions, then you'll understand why I had to do it."

"I don't think so," Billy answered.

Uncle Joe just drove along in silence for a long time chewing his plug of Brown Mule, and then he spat a stream of tobacco juice out of the window of the truck and wiped his chin with a handkerchief from the bib of his Union overalls.

"I never had nothin' in my life before I met Judge Spencer Tolliver," Joe Bradley said. "I was just a snot-nosed kid when I asked for the job at the cotton mill, and I hadn't had anything but turnip greens and sowbelly on my plate and a hunk of cornbread for breakfast, dinner, and supper. My daddy used to beat us kids every time he come home drunk, and then he beat our Ma for good measure. He was one sorry son-of-a-bitch, but my Ma wouldn't leave him. I guess she was scared he'd find her again and kill her. He killed her anyways...years and years of abuse and neglect, and she died coughing her lungs out. He was drunk at her funeral."

Joe Bradley's face contorted and Billy James could see he was trying not to cry. It made him uncomfortable.

"I'm going to tell you something I ain't never told nobody else," Uncle Joe said. "I was the oldest child in the family. I had to learn responsibility early because my daddy didn't take responsibility for anything but his whiskey, and he kept on mistreatin' us kids after Ma died.

One time he was drunk and he come home and went out to the barn to sleep it off. I come up from the field where I had been choppin' cotton. I saw him lyin' there in the corn crib with his mouth open and the flies buzzing around the puke on his shirt and I thought to myself that he was too damn sorry to live any longer."

Uncle Joe stopped the truck on the side of the road, got the water jug, filled up the tin cup, and passed it over to Billy. "You go ahead and drink first," he said.

Billy took a sip from the cup and passed it back to Uncle Joe.

"One thing you got to learn," Uncle Joe said, "is to drink a lot of water. It purifies your system." Billy James nodded. Uncle Joe finished the cup, filled it again, and passed it back to Billy. He drank as much as he could and poured the balance out of the window.

"Well," Uncle Joe said, "he was just lyin' there, passed out cold. I walked over to the hay pile, and I got a match and struck it on the wall, and I dropped it down on the floor at the edge of the hay."

Uncle Joe's eyes were on the road, but it looked like they weren't blinking. It was as if he were seeing something on a picture show screen.

"I watched that match ketch on to the chaff on the floor and crawl right onto the haystack. Then, the hay kind of made a whoofing sound as a gust of wind came in the door. I looked at my mean old daddy lying there. He never changed expression until the flames got his clothes on fire, then, he started to cough and choke. I ran out of there and down to the cotton patch. I watched that old barn go up in a sheet of flame higher than them pine trees…"

Uncle Joe pointed out of the window, "and I never saw my daddy come out. Folks all said he was drunk and set hisself afire with a cigarette, but I knew different. I knew different all these years…and I ain't never said nothing to nobody but you."

Uncle Joe started the truck and looked back behind them. He saw he had a clear space and pulled back on the road. "I did it for my brothers and sisters," he said. "I just left that hoe in the cotton patch and went over to the mill, and I asked the judge if I could work for him. He knew about the fire and knew I needed help. He gave me a chance, and I fed the family until they could make it on their own."

Uncle Joe worked up another good mouthful of spit and let it fly out the window, then wiped his chin on the handkerchief.

"Judge Spencer Tolliver saved my family from starvation. He promoted me from one thing to another, and I worked harder than anybody in the mill, and he recognized that fact. What I'm sayin' to you, Billy James, is that I had to do what I had to do. There weren't no choice for me…and a man can keep a secret when there ain't no choice."

Billy James put an arm around Lectric. The dog tried to wag his tail but couldn't because there wasn't room on the seat of the pickup truck, so he just stuck out his big, wet tongue and licked Billy on the face. It felt comforting.

Uncle Joe explained to Billy's mama about him getting homesick and wanting to come back home. "I sure am sorry about all of this," he told Billy's mama. "The boy seemed to be having a good time, but then he sort of got emotional, I guess you could say. I think it's because he's missing his daddy and all."

Billy's mama looked at him, smiled kind of sad, and said she was glad to have him back.

"I hope you don't mind me giving him the dog," Uncle Joe said. "It seemed to cheer him up quite a bit."

"I appreciate all you've done," his mama said. She tuned up to cry, and Uncle Joe put an arm around her.

"Now I don't want you worryin'," he said. "The fact is that things will always work out, one way or another."

"For them that love the Lord," she said.

After Uncle Joe had gone, Billy's mama pulled him close. "Listen to me son. It don't matter how hard times are around here…there'll come a day when everything will work out right. You may think it ain't never going to come, but God will find a way."

Billy's Ma said that a lot of the time.

Chapter 24

Mattie Herndon finished packing the boxes that represented her personal effects from 17 years in the employ of Judge Spencer Tolliver. She packed the baby pictures of Darnelle and put them in one of the suitcases. She put Darnelle's outdated clothes in a separate box for Mrs. Jacobs. She knew that some school-aged child would benefit from the well-made dresses and winter coats.

The judge came home for lunch. "What's going on here, Mattie?"

"Your lunch is on the table," she said.

"That's not what I asked."

"Your lunch is on the table.... but you'll need to get someone to clean up after because I won't be here."

The judge turned purple and looked as if he might choke. "I demand to know what is going on here!"

"I'm leaving...going to Opelika to see my folks."

"Well, this is quite sudden, isn't it? I mean, you have a right to see your folks, but..."

"I won't be coming back," Mattie said.

"You're crazy! You can't leave this place. What in hell has got into you? What about Darnelle...what in hell are you talking about, woman?"

"I have no place here anymore," Mattie said. "It's all wiped clean. All wiped clean by one insane and vicious act of hatred that you orchestrated."

The judge looked as if someone had kicked him in the stomach, but he tried hard to control his emotions. "I don't understand…"

"No, you wouldn't," Mattie said. "You're too close to your past, too close to the slaveholding ancestors who spawned your brand of hatred."

"Now listen…"

"No!" Mattie said. Will YOU please listen for once." She placed a napkin by his plate and stepped back to inspect the table. There was a tranquil sort of sadness on her face. "I have come to realize the value of a day, the worth of a moment, and I no longer find value in living under the same roof with a person who hates my race, hates my color, even hates his child…"

"NO!" The judge's voice rose sharply, "Not true!"

"I'll give you the benefit of the doubt," Mattie said, "but you can't convince me anymore."

"It was for her," the judge cried. "Don't you see? It was for HER!"

"It was because the men were COLORED, " Mattie said. "They were colored. Yes, they deserved to be punished, but it should have been in a court of law. But even that court might have a "whites only" sign…like the water fountain in your courthouse lobby?"

The judge shook his head in exasperation. "Would you have wanted all this to be dragged about in court, brought before all the prying eyes in Bogart County? Had some nigger lawyer from New York City pleading the case for these poor, underprivileged colored folks? Ruin Darnelle's life with all the publicity? Hell, NO!"

"But the OTHERS, Judge…the two women who had no part in it, and you killed them anyway…because they were COLORED!"

"NO! Because they were THERE! They were witnesses…"

Mattie felt the strength draining from her body, but her mind wouldn't permit her to stop.

"I believe I see the basis of your argument," she said. "It all comes back to the fact that you couldn't stand to have the light of day reveal your dalliance with a Negro housekeeper. You couldn't have a courtroom full of spectators nudging each other and whispering about the judge's daughter. I've come to realize the value of a day, Mr. Spencer. There have been 17 long years of days devoted to your service…"

"What about all I've done…" the judge began, but Mattie stopped him with an upraised hand. The judge was startled by her impudence.

"Oh yes, you have done as much as your heart would allow you to do," she said. "You gave me creature comforts and good food and rare moments of intimacy, but when I consider all of that…the price was too high. I gave up my family in Opelika, forfeited any chance for marriage, for real love…"

"You never asked to leave…"

"No, I didn't. I wasn't strong enough to…to give up what you offered, but did you think me less human because my skin was dark? That I was devoid of feelings?"

"Mattie, you know I never considered you to be…"

"A nigger, Mr. Spencer? Oh no…it's the old Southern paradox. You can tolerate, perhaps even feel affection for an individual of color, but still hate the race."

The judge was silent. He walked over and stood by the kitchen window. He looked off into the distance, and for a faint second, Mattie felt a twinge of pity.

"What about Darnelle?" he finally asked.

"Oh…you mean your daughter? You never acknowledged her, Mr. Spencer. You wouldn't allow her to come to your precious picnic. We had to use discretion so none of your bigoted friends might notice how much she resembles Spencer, Jr. We had to be careful, Mr. Spencer, that your son not show affection that was unseemly because you never told him that Darnelle was his sister." Mattie reached for the suitcase, and old Pike was suddenly in the hallway door.

"I'll carry the bags, Miss Mattie. You go on to the car." He didn't look at the judge for permission.

Mattie turned back to face Spencer Tolliver, and he actually seemed to be in pain. "Darnelle will be all right, Mr. Spencer. She'll go on to school and study voice and have a real life, not the shadow life that you provided. She'll be all right." She was walking then, and the words came floating back over her shoulder.

"You will never change, Mr. Spencer. You will always look at Negroes and see a long line of us stretching back to a Dark Continent, clanking our chains and moaning. That day is past, Mr. Spencer' it's over…and it will never happen again!"

The judge was turning purple with rage, but Mattie didn't care. She looked at him as if he was made of a thin sheet of cotton. She looked at him and through him and walked toward the door. "No, you'll never change, Mr. Spencer. The world will change around you and leave you behind…leave you fixed in time…with nothing but your hatred to sustain you."

"Out of my house!" the judge screamed, "Out, you ungrateful…impudent…hussy! Get out…get OUT!"

But Mattie was gone, and the words fell around him, brittle word sounds that cracked and splintered against the high walls and ceilings and fell into the empty silence of the mansion.

Chapter 25

The judge never saw Mattie Lou Herndon again. He did see his daughter, Darnelle, however. She came to Mulberry on a fine October afternoon in 1956, riding in a hired limousine, all the way from Atlanta.

The housekeeper, Essie Livingston, answered the ring at the big front door, and her eyes got round with amazement when she saw the long, white limo in the graveled drive. The young lady at the door was dressed in stylish sportswear and had a foreign look to her. She asked if the Tolliver boys were at home and the housekeeper shook her head.

"How about his honor, the judge?"

"Yes'm. He here, but he don't see peoples he don't know."

"He knows me," Darnelle said.

"Yes?" the judge questioned his visitor, then, he recognized Darnelle. They stood there awkwardly without speaking.

"May I come in?" she asked.

"Of course, er, of course you can." The judge pulled the door wide and Darnelle walked into the familiar front hall.

"Come in the study," the judge said, "and I'll have Essie bring us some lemonade."

"I could use something stronger, if it's not too much trouble," she said.

"A sherry?"

"That would be nice." Darnelle sat in one of the old wing backed chairs and nursed the sherry on her knee. "So, where are the boys?"

The judge cleared his throat and reached for his drink. "Spencer is dead, and Michael might as well be, for all I'll ever know of him."

Darnelle's face lost some of its studied aloofness.

"How did it happen?"

"Oh, the Korean war, of course, in Spencer's case. Michael is another story."

"Tell me about it?"

"Not that much to tell. I gave him the cotton mill business, and he sold it to Arondale Mills. Took his money and ran."

"To where?"

"To as God forsaken a place as he could think of, I suppose. He went to Alaska."

"Poor Spencer…"

"They say he never knew what hit him…I'm grateful for that…but I've lost both my sons."

"And someone else," Darnelle said quietly.

"My mother. Mattie Lou…"

"I know her name," the judge interrupted.

"I'm sure that you do," Darnelle said, "but you had no knowledge of her death did you?"

The judge shook his head. He was visibly shaken.

"I…didn't know…"

Darnelle's face grew cold and aloof once more. "She died of a heart attack, so the doctor's say. I know she died of a broken heart, too. You see, she loved someone who couldn't return her love…couldn't acknowledge that she existed in the daylight hours."

"Now stop that," the judge said.

Darnelle rose from her chair and put the sherry glass down on the lamp table.

"You didn't acknowledge her, and you didn't acknowledge me." The judge rose to his feet also. They stood apart from each other, each on guard from the other, like two wild beasts of prey.

"I have paid your bills for a long time,' he said finally.

"And I have come to pay you back," she said, as she reached for her purse.

The judge backed away as if he sensed she might be reaching for a weapon. It was a checkbook, instead. Darnelle reached inside and snapped out the check she had already written. "It's for thirty-five thousand, six hundred and forty-one dollars," she said. "Every penny that you ever spent."

"I didn't ask to be repaid," the judge said.

"No, you didn't. Just say it's my desire to have no obligation to you."

"How did you come by that amount of money?" the judge asked.

"Well, I didn't sell my body, if that's what you're thinking. I sell my voice though. I'm a singer."

"Please sit down," the judge said.

"Could I have another?"

"You're not a drinker, are you?"

Darnelle laughed then, a spontaneous, hearty laugh that reminded him of Spencer, Jr. "No, not one of those either."

"I don't even know where you live," he said.

"In Paris. I live in Paris now, but I'll be moving to the French countryside soon. I'm getting married."

"To a Frenchman?"

"Yes. You'd approve his color."

"Now, I don't find that appropriate..."

"Oh, I think you do. I think color is always appropriate for your consideration."

"I may ask you to leave," the judge threatened.

Darnelle rose once again and placed the glass and the check on the lamp table. "I'm leaving, Judge." She reached into her handbag and pulled out a newspaper clipping. The judge could see it was from the Atlanta Journal. He didn't subscribe to the Journal because he didn't approve of the liberal editorial pages. "Thought this might interest you," she said.

He looked at her picture and, then, the name under it.

"Who is this?"

"Me…it's me, Judge, my name…known throughout the civilized world. I made up my own you see, when you didn't give me one."

"I don't see why you have to be so argumentative."

"No, you never allowed argument, did you, Judge? I guess you could say that I'm one of those uppity niggers." She gulped down the last of the sherry. "Do you still shoot uppity niggers in Bogart County?"

"I must ask you to go," he said.

She swept out of the door and got into the limo. The driver eased down the drive. She didn't look back.

The judge watched her go. He stood in the doorway and watched the limo out of sight. Then, he walked inside and picked up the check, ripped it into bits, and put them into the fireplace. He put the newspaper clipping with his important papers in the wall safe beside the letter from Franklin Delano Roosevelt.

Chapter 26
1997

Billy James Bradley celebrated his 62nd birthday in a vacation lodge near Denver, Colorado. The lodge was a temporary stopover on a trip that he had contemplated making for thirty years. He was going back to Mulberry, Georgia.

He was newly retired from his position with California Chemical and was recently widowed. A long time ago, he had returned briefly to his hometown of Augusta, Georgia. That was after his Viet Nam tour of duty. He had come back to stay but found he couldn't forget Donna, the stunning, California girl that he had dated in San Francisco.

He went back to California, married the girl and went to work for California Chemical, which was her father's company, and he stayed there for 30 years, the last 10 of them as a vice president in production.

He had two grown children, both gainfully employed and now he suddenly found himself without responsibility for anyone or anything other than himself. This lack of a daily schedule bothered him considerably. He had learned over the years that work was his best friend. As long as there was enough work, enough responsibility, there was no time for him to dwell on the event that had haunted him throughout his early years of life.

And there was the problem with the great vacuum in his soul. He realized that over a span of many years of marriage, you make adjustments to the partner who shares your life. You adjust to their thought processes and they to yours. You adjust to physical differences, to moral opinions, to matters of faith and charity.

Suddenly, that part of your life is over and there are no adjustments to make. You recognize that you served as a composite structure and not a complete entity. You no longer recognize the half- person that is you. You have to learn, in some fashion, to become whole once more, and this he knew, would be a difficult undertaking.

His children were aware of the changed condition, the complete futility of trying to make a mother AND father of the person left to them. They sensed the change but were not aware perhaps, of the daunting complexities facing the survivor parent. They wanted only to remember the role the parent had played in all the years before. He couldn't reprise that role because the star of the show was gone, and he knew that he had just been the second banana.

He had to find an identity that was satisfactory to his own sense of worthiness. He knew that one's self-image was crucial to the art of survival. He wondered if he should now take the time to search for the faith that had given his widowed mother the strength to rear her poor, fatherless children.

And not just rear them, but provide them the security of unfailing love throughout their formative years. She made no secret of the fact that she relied on God's mercy and support. "Don't worry son," she would say, " there'll come a day when everything will work out fine. You may think it ain't never coming, but things work out for them that love the Lord."

Billy James Bradley thought more about his mother in the past year than in all the years since her death. He hadn't understood her needs, had not in fact ever considered them. He supposed it was the nature of youth to be chiefly concerned about one's own welfare.

Somewhere out there, he hoped to find the right answers. The trip back to Mulberry was a beginning.

He wasn't in a hurry to go back to where the problem began. In fact, he wanted desperately to avoid going back, but there was a compulsion to go and he knew in his heart that he would have to do it. He thought he could defer it a bit and maybe even get back to normal by heading out to Colorado for some fishing and golfing and exploring.

It wasn't working though. The dreams came back to him even on his vacation retreat, and so he was awake at 4 o'clock in the morning.

He read the newspaper and turned on the television set. The news was not encouraging and the weather prediction even worse. There would be rain and more rain over the next few days. The rain came in slender crystal threads that unraveled from the dark roll of cloud above the mountain. It fell down through the tops of the evergreens to the leafy floor of the forest below.

Billy James could look up and see the rain coming and he could look down and see it falling, and he felt like he was suspended somewhere between the ground and the sky. He watched television and he drank Canadian Club and he watched the rain for three days and three nights. Then he said to hell with it and called a cab.

He didn't know why he decided to go back to Mulberry by Greyhound Bus. Maybe because he was in no hurry, maybe because he hoped he might work out an answer in time to avoid the final destination. In any case, he told the cab driver to take him to the bus station.

"Where to?" the lady behind the counter asked.

"Georgia," Billy James said, "get me a bus going in the direction of Georgia."

"I got one going to New Orleans in thirty minutes," she said. "I'll take that one," he said.

Billy remembered the first time he had ridden on a Greyhound bus. He was seventeen at the time and a senior high school student and he rode the bus all the way to Miami, Florida. He could still recall the road signs advertising alligator farms and SNAKEATORIUMS, the latter being a word that guaranteed instant, shivering response.

That year he grew a mustache and secretly added a little mascara to the growth to enhance the color. The girls at Augusta High compared him to Turhan Bey, who was a matinee idol at the Rialto Theatre at the time.

He slicked his hair back with 'brilliantine' and he purchased two shirts for the trip that were made of shiny, synthetic material. One of the shirts was red and the other was yellow, and both of them were unbearably hot in the Florida sunshine. He wore the collars out over his tan sport jacket and knew that he looked pretty good. He had stopped in one of the terminal photo booths and put quarters in the machine and it spat out numerous sepia toned likenesses that he mailed to the girls back home.

He had fifty dollars in his pocket for the trip that he had made picking cotton and it felt like a fortune in the new leather billfold that his Ma had gotten him for graduation.

He remembered the girl he met on that trip. She had long, silky blonde hair that fell over one eye and the other eye was the deepest blue he had ever seen.

Billy James was on his way back home and the girl got on the bus at the Miami terminal. She had a straw hat with a bright scarf band and she had a small overnight bag in her hand. She stopped right next to where he was seated by the window and looked up and down the aisle as if she hadn't noticed the empty seat beside him.

"Is this seat taken, sir?" she had asked and his mind had disintregated into flotsam. He finally shook his head, feeling his face flush and knowing that she considered him to be an idiot. She placed the overnight bag in the rack overhead and he had tried to rise to help and instead bumped his head on the rack and floundered back into a sitting position.

She removed the hat and placed it in her lap and introduced herself. He managed to give his own name and sat in rigid silence for the next twenty miles.

They got together at the next rest stop and ordered grilled cheese sandwiches. She ordered a coke and he, with all the assurance he could muster, ordered a beer. The mustache must have been the remedy because they didn't ask for his age or ID.

The incomparable Ink Spots were doing "Gypsy" on the jukebox and after the beer, Billy began to sing along with them and when he got to the words 'she can look in the future and drive away all your fears' he was suddenly fearless himself.

They got back on the bus and in a feat of unbelievable daring, he reached for her hand and kissed her lightly on the cheek. He immediately panicked, but then she smiled at him so tenderly in the faint light from the lamps overhead and leaned her face toward him. He kissed her proffered lips and fell into bottomless ecstasy.

They smooched all the way to her destination in Tallahassee and Billy would have liked to have gotten off and spent the rest of his life making love to her, but his Ma needed him back home, and he never saw her again.

Today there was a vacant seat next to a man dressed in cowboy attire, Wrangler jeans, curled brim hat and boots with slanted heels that had seen better days. The cowboy looked as if he had been in the company of the boots for a long time. Billy took the vacant space and the cowboy lifted the brim of the hat enough to acknowledge his presence.

"Did you ever think a man could drop out of civilization for 20 years?" The cowboy was talking and Billy James looked around but it was apparent the cowboy was speaking to him.

"I'm not sure I get the picture," he said.

"He was my oldest brother and he was the first to leave the farm. He went off to the university and nobody expected him to come back out to the sticks. He did though, came back when my Ma died and back again when Pa died in the nursing home."

The cowboy's face took on a mournful look, his expressions slipping easily in the creases of it, from happy to sad, a versatile and honest face that moved with and accented his words.

"He got some military training while he was in college and I guess a career in the army was an opportunity for him- he didn't have any connections or anything, you see.

All the rest of us found other ways to make a living," the cowboy grinned, "or ways to starve to death, tryin to make a living.

Well the old farmhouse just stood there after Pa died and the grass and briars grew over the fields. My brother kept the taxes paid, even when he was in the service, and after Viet Nam he took his retirement from the army and came back home."

The cowboy shifted in his seat and stared out of the bus window for a while.

"I guess we didn't communicate much after our parents died and none of us knew about his falling in love with one of those Asian girls while he was overseas. He had written it all down in his diary, and I was the one found it when we heard he had died.

I went back to that old house and went through things with my younger brother and our married sister. The diary was in an old footlocker. Just about everything in that old house had been stolen during the time it stood vacant and it looked like my brother had furnished it out of army surplus."

The cowboy shook his head, the face smiling easily now as he recalled the scene. "Can you believe he didn't even own a TV? The only news he got was when he went into town for supplies. I don't know what really happened to him overseas but it must have been pretty traumatic. He wouldn't talk about the war at all, according to the folks back home. Just kept to himself out there, made a little hay for a milk cow and a horse and he had a German Shepherd dog.

He'd come into town for supplies and he'd stop off at the beer joint on the way home and have a few cold ones. He never got into no trouble, well no real trouble. The town folks said there was a feller once got to feelin his oats a little and he come up to my brother and mouthed off and my brother just looked at him sort of sad like. He said ' go on home to yore Mama boy' and he stared at that boy til he dropped his head and got on out of there."

Billy James nodded, " It seems like he must have had some tough times."

"Well I guess so," the cowboy said. "He was with the Rangers and I reckon he made a good one." He grinned again. "Looks like the good old U.S. Army has always found some hazardous duty for us Native Americans."

Billy James said he wasn't aware the man was an Indian.

"Well, you'd have thought so if you could have seen my brother. Now he was really dark- like my Mama. My Dad, he was white, but my Mama's people came out here in the Creek removal. She had connections all the way back to Chief Eufaula."

Billy was interested. His own Mama had told him she had Indian blood.

"My brother had a lot of books on Indian history," the cowboy said. "I think he must have spent most of his spare time reading when he wasn't writing appeals to the army or to congress or anyone that might help him to find that Asian girl."

"You mean she got left behind?"

"Yeah. When the Commies moved in, things got very confused and he wasn't allowed to take her with him. Who can say what happened to a girl that had been connected with an American soldier?

I let my sister keep all the personal effects. I ain't got much room in my travel trailer, if you know what I mean. My younger brother, he works for Sam Walton's company. I've heard Sam was the richest man in the country at the time he died. Anyway, my younger brother, he didn't want anything."

The cowboy grinned again. "Nah- I'm just an ole rodeo cowboy- all I've ever done. Worked the rodeos most of my adult life. Guess I'll keep at it til I get too broke up to handle it anymore. I didn't want nothin he had –ceptin this here-" He reached in his jacket pocket and pulled out a yellowed envelope. He reached inside and pulled out a small circle of blue satin with white stars embossed in the bottom and a gold medallion shaped to form the head of Minerva, the Roman Goddess Of War. It was the Congressional Medal of honor.

"Now that's the highest honor they give a man," the cowboy said. He handed it to Billy James and Billy held it in his hand, admiring its beauty and knowing full well the valorous conduct that it represented.

The cowboy's face creased easily back into a smile, the skin texture loose and pliable as if it had been kneaded and scrubbed with saddle soap. "The white man used to buy Indian land and Indian women and hides and stuff with trinkets. Indians just naturally like jewelry, shiny stuff like that, or any kind of ornamentation. Guess I ain't no different."

He took the medal and folded it carefully back into the envelope.

"Nobody ever knew he had it. I didn't even know that it was his until I read the citation about being above and beyond the call of duty. I think I'll hang on to this."

"I sure don't blame you," Billy James said.

Chapter 27

Billy rode straight through to Oklahoma City, through little towns in eastern Oklahoma with rolling hills and green pastures. He could see people from the window of the bus and they were coming into town for Saturday shopping and they would go to Wal-Mart and visit on the sidewalks. He supposed the population was descended from the inheritors of the Land Rush, the Greeks and Italians and English and Irish and Germans and the survivors of the Dust Bowl. And the children of the original inhabitants walked among them, those citizens of Alabama and Georgia, driven to the land by a promise from the government of the United States that the land would be theirs so long as the grass should grow.

It was Saturday and the sun was shining and he was hot and thirsty. He made his way to the first beer joint in walking distance of the bus station.

There was one empty chair at a table occupied by an oil field worker. His hard hat said Kerr Oil on the front and the hat's owner gave Billy a straightforward, appraising look and Billy nodded. The man was drinking from one bottle with a full one on standby. He pushed the full one toward Billy. "Have a Coors," he said as if he wouldn't take no for an answer.

"Don't mind if I do," Billy said, "and I'll get the next round." The oilman nodded and leaned back in his chair.

"Now you take old Jim Bakker," the oilman wiped a hand across his beer- frothed mustaches. "Now he wasn't that damn bad of a feller, all things considered."

"Whatever happened to him?"

"Well he served time, you know. Yeah, he probably wouldn't kill a cockroach but he had to serve time and a good lawyer can get a killer turned loose slick as a whistle."

He looked at Billy for confirmation and Billy had the feeling that most of the time the oil man got ready agreement on whatever topic he picked. The fierce features and the righteous delivery of his pronouncements called for agreement and Billy nodded.

"Fact is- all those people who sent in money to the Jim and Tammy show really wanted to do it. They wanted to do good and it made them feel like they were DOING good. I ain't arguing that Old Jim didn't live it up some nor that Tammy didn't enjoy the fruits of her tearful performances, but the fact is- the public enjoyed it too."

The oilman took another long pull from the bottle and nodded. " So here is everybody enjoying what they're doing and then what happens?"

"I heard he got caught with a secretary," Billy said.

The oilman turned in his chair to hail the waitress, who was already being summoned by other patrons. "Hey Wanda- get my buddy and me some more beer!"

The waitress came with the beer and Billy paid and the oilman gave her two extra dollars. "Here now, put one of them in the juke box. We need to hear some Willie or Waylon-"

"It's Willie AND Waylon and me," she said.

"Well hell babe, I'll take you anytime, but in the meantime play us a little music on the jukebox." The oilman gave her a playful slap on her fanny and turned again to the issue at hand.

"Like I was saying, any time you got a whole bunch of people, all having a good time, then something is bound to happen. Nine times out of ten, it's going to be the old sex monster. Yep, sure as shootin, that old rascal is going to raise up his horny head and make problems for somebody . All of old Jim Bakker's cards came tumbling down for one reason and that old sex monster was responsible. Do you follow what I'm saying?"

"I believe that I do," Billy said.

"Yes sir, that's what happened and it damned sure ain't the first time either. Remember Elmer Gantry? Now that was a good movie. Old Burt Lancaster was the best, fit the part to a tee.

I talked to one of them revival preachers once. He told me they are cautioned in the divinity schools to be wary of the sex monster. Same thing with doctors and lawyers. Women just go for them. It's the power thing. A female creature is dependent, as it were, on the men who directly influence the life she now enjoys, or the life she may have after death. And she wants to get closer to that influence and affect it in a positive manner. You follow me?"

"It's getting a little deep for a Saturday afternoon," Billy said.

The oilman affected a look of deep concentration that caused his brow to furrow and the mustaches to droop lower.

"I think we have to ask ourselves if it was really a back rub that old Jim wanted and by the same token, was the secretary really under the impression she was going to get religious instruction?" The oilman suddenly sat upright and belched loudly and winked in Billy's direction. "The condition that confronts you and me on this lovely summer afternoon is how we can find some sweet and desirable creature who wants to be influenced in a positive manner. You follow me?"

Billy told him the point was well taken but that his bus was leaving within the hour and this wouldn't allow him enough time to pursue the matter. He would be obliged if the oilman would carry on the quest in his absence.

The oilman studied Billy carefully and then the beer frothed mustaches lifted and spread out with his grin. "You're all right Dude," he said.

The waitress was bringing another Coors and Billy rose and excused himself. "Watch out for that sex monster," he said.

The jukebox came alive with Merle Haggard's voice, wondering if the good times were really over for good. Billy had a feeling they might be.

Chapter 28

The woman in the seat next to him was in her sixties, smallish and prim and she talked in the manner of one accustomed to stating facts that refuted any opposition.

"I've lived in the South all of my life," she said. "I've never been further west than this point in Oklahoma and this will be my last trip here. I wouldn't have come this time but Bertha- she's my niece- is moving soon to Alaska and it's a fact that I'll never make it up there. She's a geologist you know. No, I've no plans to travel north but I would like to see the Florida Keys."

She rendered this information as if Billy James had requested a statement of her position on travel and having spoken reached into a cardboard box labeled Kentucky Fried Chicken and selected a drumstick.

"Would you like a piece of chicken?" she asked, smiling now as she held up the drumstick for his inspection.

"Why no," he said, "I just left a food- just had something," he managed.

"My impression is that you have been indulging in strong drink and I do hope that you are eating properly."

Billy was somewhat shaken by the accusation and a quick flush of resentment was his immediate response but then he looked more closely at the woman and seeing no reproach in her expression, deduced she was indeed concerned about his welfare.

"Sure you won't have one of these?" she asked, "and just look at the size of the biscuits!"

Billy smiled then and accepted the biscuit and a drumstick. He thought he hadn't tasted anything quite so good since he left home. He chewed hungrily and the lady finished her chicken and wiped her fingers on one of the damp towels in the box. She handed one of the towels to Billy and continued her recital.

"My parents never left Memphis, Tennessee. They bought groceries from the first self-serve market in the United States. Do you know what it was called?"

Billy confessed he had no clue.

"It was the Piggly Wiggly store and it opened for business back in 1916. Most of the people I meet know of Memphis because of Elvis Presley. They don't realize it's one of the world's largest inland markets for hardwood lumber and the meat- packing center of the south."

"I never knew that," Billy stated.

"Oh yes, Hernando de Soto raised his flag in Memphis and Andrew Jackson once owned the place. It was wiped out by the Yellow Fever in 1878. It has been called the city of churches and it is a leading medical research center."

"Oh yeah," Billy said, " that girl, uh, her father was what's his name- St. Jude Hospital-"

"It was Danny Thomas and his daughter was Marlo. She married Donohue."

"I knew that," Billy James said.

"Sometimes, if one imbibes too much, it becomes difficult to remember small but important details."

"I'm glad you have no problem with that," Billy said.

"Well, I certainly don't. People always ask me, 'have you been to Graceland?'

I say, "yes I have- but there's more to Memphis than Graceland. We've come a long way in the past fifty years. Much change has taken place and most of it for the better."

The woman lowered her voice and looked around the bus. "You know there was a time when nobody but white folks rode up in the front of the bus. When the bus stopped there would be rest rooms marked MEN and WOMEN and then one other that said COLORED. The black men and women and children all had to share that one rest room. And they couldn't come into the restaurant to eat. They had to order from the window and eat outside."

She sat for a moment and said "I know now that was wrong, but I have to say that I just wasn't aware how wrong it was. It was just the way things had always been. I certainly never considered that my children would attend a public school that was integrated."

"I suppose we all decide the morality of a situation according to the way it affects us personally," Billy said.

"Well, I never thought about it that way," the lady said. "But you know, morality has to work the same for everybody." She smiled ruefully, and almost as if she was thinking out loud posed a question. "What do you think the media would have to say about a United White College Fund or a Miss WHITE America contest? How about a WHITE Music Awards show?"

"They wouldn't have many complimentary things to say," Billy ventured.

"No they wouldn't- but it's all right to have separate schools, separate beauty pageants, separate race history classes, separate professional arts awards…it all right to do these things, but only if you are black."

She glanced out the window at the countryside, seeing the magnolias shimmering white under the branches of the taller trees and the green pastures rushing by the windows. "I just think the summertime is a marvelous season for travel," she said.

"You make a good point," Billy James said, still thinking about the morality of the separate schools and contests.

The woman gave him a quizzical look and elected not to pursue the conversation. She opened a copy of The Ladies Home Journal.

"I really appreciated that fried chicken," Billy said.

"You are quite welcome," she replied.

He called a cab from the bus station in New Orleans. The cab smelled of vomit and his shoes stuck to the carpeting in the rear. He dreaded to think of the fearful condition of the trunk where the driver had deposited his suitcase.

"Where to Mon?" the driver asked from the rear view mirror. His droopy eyelids were barely open and the chauffeur's cap failed to seat over the dreadlock hairstyle.

"Bourbon Street," Billy said, because he had never been there even though he had heard of the street all of his adult life. "Find me a hotel with a decent room for the night."

The driver made no reply and gunned the cab into the traffic. The doors rattled on their hinges and the whole of the cab vibrated like the threshing machine his uncle had operated back in Mulberry, Georgia. Billy decided the driver was either drunk, high on drugs, or both.

"Slow this thing down!" he yelled to the front seat.

"You want out Mon?"

"I want you to slow down."

The driver grunted without acknowledging the request and they finally careened around a corner and slid to a halt in front of an old brick building with an ironwork balustrade around the porches.

"This yo stop Mon. Twenty Seven fifty."

The driver lifted the bag from the trunk and Billy entered the building. A dark faced woman with long, black hair tied up in the back looked up from her magazine.

"I'd like a room, please."

The woman slid a card across the counter. He filled it out and handed it back to her and she said it was seventy- five plus tax. He paid it in cash and took his bag to the elevator and went up to the second floor. He decided the carpeting in the corridor came from the same roll as the cab because his shoes stuck to the fabric as he walked.

When he opened the door he was greeted by a stale fragrance left by a previous guest. He walked to a window and opened it and stood there while the air conditioner labored at exchanging the air.

Billy James' reaction to New Orleans was mainly olfactory in the summer night. There were sticky sweet smells of wine and mixed drinks and sour smells of rotting salads. Revelers strolled on the street, swinging beer bottles and a country boy set up a series of howls while another voice hollered "Go Dogs!" Billy had to think you could find a Georgia Bulldog fan just about any-where.

By contrast, the morning dawned bright and beautiful. Mer-chants hosed down sidewalks in front of their shops. A few late stragglers made their way back to homes or hotels. The birds sang and the sun's warm rays touched the spires of the St. Louis Ca-thedral and danced in the ripples of the waterfront.

He stopped in at the Café du Monde and had beignets and coffee, and he watched the sidewalk artists working at their easels and he listened to a black man play the trumpet. He was glad that he had come to New Orleans.

Chapter 29

The fat man at the bus station in Mobile, Alabama stirred powdered creamer into his coffee. He shoved a copy of a newspaper across the table to Billy, pointing to a picture on the obituary page. The picture was of a lady apparently in her late fifties, with straight, silver colored hair.

"They called her 'Mailbox Annie," the man said. "She went off her rocker several years back. Fancied herself to be a writer and I guess she was. She carried stuff she had written to the post office and sent it off to publishing houses. They sent it all back or most of it I reckon and she just kept right at it anyway.

She went down to that post office every single day to check her mailbox, and then she'd go up to the counter and inquire if they might have overlooked some of her mail. "I'm expecting a letter from my publisher," she would say.

The waitress approached their table and sat a plate of sliced red tomatoes in front of the fat man. "Your bacon and eggs will be coming up in a minute," she said.

She looked at Billy and smiled pleasantly and he suddenly realized he hadn't looked at the menu, so he just said, "bring me the same."

"You want the tomatoes too?"

"Oh yeah, they look good."

The fat man nodded but waited for the bacon and eggs before touching the tomatoes.

"A long time ago, the lady was a school teacher. A good one so they say. Didn't get married 'til she was in her forties. Met this feller who was with one of the fertilizer companies. He traveled through this part of the state and they say he met her right here at this bus station.

After that, seems she was going off to New Orleans for vacation. She went someplace every summer when school was out. One time she went all the way to Los Angeles, California. When she'd come back, she'd share all her trip experiences with the children she taught in her geography class.

Well this feller- fertilizer salesman, he struck up a conversation with her. Said he was going to New Orleans himself and would she like somebody with experience to show her around the city. She said she thought that was mighty accommodating. Well sir, she didn't share that trip experience with the geography class. She did start to go to New Orleans on a right regular basis after that."

The waitress brought a plate of steaming scrambled eggs and grits and put it in front of the fat man. "Yours'll be up in just a minute," she said.

"No rush," Billy said, "I've got plenty of time."

The fat man took a loaded fork full of the eggs and continued. " The fertilizer salesman came home with Miss Annie one day. Moved right into that big old house she inherited from her mother. Course that's why she hadn't married sooner- she took care of her mother, who was ailing for nigh on to twenty years, I guess. Between taking care of her and teaching school, she just didn't have time for no feller until the fertilizer salesman came along.

I reckon that's why she took it so hard when he up and left her. Some say they was never married in the first place because he had a wife and kids in Louisiana. I don't know. You know how people are- like to talk and surmise a situation."

The man took another good mouthful and chewed on one side of his mouth and talked out of the other. "Anyway, he was there one day and he was gone the next and before long, Miss Annie, she gave up the teaching job and went off out to Arkansas to one of them sanitariums or something. When she come back, she was still friendly but it was a kind of a put-on, if you know what I mean.

A real gracious lady though. I used to cut grass for her when I was in high school. She would invite me to have some iced tea or a sandwich or something. One time I got to her house before the dew was dry on the grass. It was a Saturday as I recall and she was settin out breakfast on the back porch.

I had left early and I think I had a box of corn flakes or something and that breakfast of hers shore looked good to me. She said "Melvin- you just pull up a chair and you help me eat this breakfast. My eyes must have been bigger than my stomach," she said.

The waitress arrived with Billy's food and it looked just like the fat man's food had looked before he mixed the eggs into the grits and poured tomato catsup over the top. She refilled Billy's coffee cup and the fat man's cup.

"Well, I have to tell you that was one fine breakfast that Miss Annie had prepared. She served me some sliced red tomatoes and I had never eaten tomatoes for breakfast before. I really took a liking to them and if its tomato season, I'm going to have me a plate with my eggs and bacon.

"Yessir, Miss Annie was a real fine lady. I guess it was sort of cruel for folks to call her "Mailbox Annie," but people are like that. Seems to make folks feel better to find fault with somebody else. I have often thought that people, taken as a group, are not too admirable. They're a lot like flocks of chickens-let one develop a sore and the rest will peck him to death. .

Anyways, the man down at the post office, he told me she got some mail just yesterday and it was from one of them publishing houses in New York City. Ain't that the way life works out though? Nothing fair about it, you might say."

The man took his fork and lifted two red ripe slices from the plate. He opened his mouth and made adjustment for the bite. He chewed with great satisfaction and swallowed noisily.

"Well, here I am, doing all the talking as usual. I guess that is common for me. How about you? Where you going?"

"I think I may go back to Georgia," Billy answered.

"You mean you don't know?"

"Well, I'm heading in that direction until I find something more interesting to do."

"Hey, that's pretty good. Guess you are one of them free spirits?'

"You could look at it that way."

Billy looked out of the window as an old blue Pontiac pulled up to the curb. It had a bumper sticker on the left front fender that read 'BOYCOTT GENERAL ELECTRIC.' It had something to do with nuclear weaponry but the print was too small to read from where he sat.

"That's something I never liked," he said, more to himself than to the fat man.

"What's that you say?"

"Bumper stickers," Billy said, " I never liked bumper stickers."

The fat man chuckled. "I saw one the other day that was a good un," he said. "I was driving along pretty close to this Ford F-150 pickup and it had a bumper sticker that you could only read when you got up close. Know what it said?"

"I can't imagine."

"It said, if you get any closer *I'll blow snot on you!*"

Billy pushed his plate aside. "That's pretty good," he said.

"No need to rush off."

"Well, I thought I'd walk around the city."

"Too bad you couldn't finish your breakfast," the fat man sympathized. "Guess you won't mind if I eat the rest of your tomatoes?"

"Not at all," Billy said, "you just help yourself."

He had strolled around the downtown area for two or three hours. He remembered reading somewhere that Mobile had been the first city in the south to have street lighting and that was back in the days before the Civil War. They were gaslights of course, and he thought the old lampposts he had seen in certain quarters harkened back to those days.

He literally bumped into the lady as he walked. She was burdened down with packages and he wasn't looking and they just collided. Billy James offered profuse apologies and bent down to help her retrieve the scattered parcels.

"No problem," the lady said, reaching for the boxes now stacked on Billy's left arm.

"Please allow me to help you to your car," Billy said.

"Oh, they still make old fashioned Southern Gentlemen?"

"Well, I was born in the south, but I've lived in California for the past thirty years."

"Okay, that still qualifies you, and yes, I'd appreciate your help. My car's just down the next block."

Billy James walked beside her and noticed she was just shorter than his shoulder and that she had straw- blonde hair tied back in a ponytail. She was in her mid-fifties and when she smiled up at him, her eyes reminded him of the ocean, bluish green and sparkling.

They reached the car and deposited the articles in the car's trunk and then Billy James stood awkwardly, wanting to find the right words for the situation and finding none.

"Are you hungry?" the lady asked.

"Starving," he lied. "I was just thinking of finding a good spot for lunch."

They went to place called Wentzels and the hostess found a booth for them.

"I remember this place from childhood," she said. "There was a sign by the cash register back then and it read ' In case of atomic attack, pay your bill, then run like hell.'

People thought that was pretty cute."

"Yeah, I guess so," he said.

They ordered oyster sandwiches, which the lady, whose name turned out to be Penelope Susan Jamison, assured him were the best on the coast.

"You can just call me Sue," she said.

They lingered over the meal and he learned that she had been a widow for the past two years and that she lived at a place called Gulf Shores, south of the city.

"I'm a retired school Marm," she explained. "My husband bought a vacation place for us some years ago down at Gulf Shores and it became a second home to me-a first home now, as it turns out."

"Where was the first home?"

"Birmingham. Have you ever been there?"

"No, it's just another of the many places that I've missed in my lifetime."

She looked at him in such a way that he found himself talking easily about his own life. He told her about the early years in Augusta and his football years at the University of Georgia and the army years. Finally he told her that he was also widowed and retired from his company.

"Where, may I ask, are you going?" she inquired.

"Back to Georgia- a sentimental journey, I suppose you could call it."

"How long will you be there?"

"I've not decided that, as yet."

He walked her back to her car. They stood there and she smiled at him.

"Well, if you're ever back in Mobile-"

"Could I have your telephone number?" he heard himself ask.

"I'm in the telephone book at Gulf Shores. You've never seen the Gulf Coast?"

"No- not been there either."

"Then you should see it- so much prettier than those California beaches. The sand is white as sugar, and there's still the feel of the '30's in the dunes and architecture."

"I think I'd like very much to see that," he said.

She waved from the car window and Billy felt a strange and forgotten tug of the heart.

He waved back and walked toward the bus terminal and sort of wished the bus were heading south instead of the opposite direction.

Chapter 30

The Atlanta terminal was crowded, even on a Sunday morning. Billy James hailed a cab and asked the driver to give him a tour of Peachtree Street.

"Which one?"

"Well, start with the main one, and circle around some."

The cabbie grinned and pulled into traffic. Billy could not believe the changes in a city that he had thought he remembered. The IBM building, the High Museum, Peachtree Center and all the grand skyscrapers that had evolved since he last saw the city left him totally bewildered.

They drove for an hour up one street and down another and out to Turner Field and over to the Atlanta Stadium and finally Billy James had the cab pull into a car rental facility.

"You did a good job for me," he told the cabbie.

"Well…put your money where your mouth is," the cab driver drawled, but his face was friendly and he grinned again when he said it. Billy nodded and paid the fare.

The expressways too, were a complete marvel. He got a map at the rental agency and they directed him to I-20 for his trip eastward from the city. He came to I-285 and was tempted to just drive around the complete circle and he decided to put that on a list of possible things to do.

He watched the progress from the window. Golf courses and apartments and condominium complexes had replaced the cotton fields he remembered on either side of old 278 to Atlanta. Off to the right of the expressway, he saw the beginnings of a great new mall in the Lithonia area and the building never stopped between that point and the charming old city of Covington. He got off at the Covington exit and drove into the old part of town that he remembered so well. He saw the refurbished courthouse, the delightful old trees on the square that were now so much larger. They furnished an umbrella of branches that reached across all four corners of the square. He drove around the block and alongside the First Presbyterian Church where Peter Marshall used to preach. He added a return visit to that new list he was making.

It had been more than fifty years, but Billy James Bradley still remembered the hollyhocks. They had grown on either side of the dirt drive that led from the highway to Uncle Joe's house. They were tall and straight and the slender stalks were full of buds. They came flashing back into his memory as if there had been no interruption of half a century.

He remembered the clustered petals, all pink and white in the sunlight. He had ridden alongside Uncle Joe in the old pickup truck with the dog in his lap, and he had watched the hollyhocks go by the window. Now he heard Uncle Joe's voice, just as plain as on that morning so long ago, "You know you can't never come back here no more, don't you, Billy James? You hear me boy? Not EVER-" and Uncle Joe's hand had tightened like a steel vise on his shoulder. Billy James had nodded his head, and because the vise got tighter, he had gasped a "yes sir."

He turned off the Interstate and headed north up Georgia Highway 11. He traveled along the paved road with the railroad on the left side and the pastures on the right. He remembered the road was graveled then, and there were rows and rows of cotton plants on either side of the road.

He saw a sign advertising the Blue Willow Inn, and it made him think of Lewis Grizzard. Before he died, Lewis wrote a folksy column in the Atlanta Journal and other papers around the country, and he appeared on Johnny Carson's show and got a lot of publicity for his humor. He was sort of a latter-day version of Will Rogers.

Anyway, Lewis liked to eat at the Blue Willow Inn. He liked to eat anywhere that quality food was served, and he wrote about the best places in his newspaper column. Billy James knew that Lewis Grizzard saw life differently than some folks, and maybe that was because he sensed that he didn't have as much time as other folks.

Billy James hadn't looked at this road in a long time. He saw the city limit sign for Social Circle. The sign said the town was founded in 1832. He remembered his uncle telling him the village had straddled the line between the Cherokee and Creek Indian nations.

He drove over the railroad bridge and looked off down to the right toward the cotton mill, only the mill wasn't there any more. There were brick corners sticking up from the burned out remains, and scattered piles of broken brick still covered the grounds. The railway station was beyond the burned out mill and was no longer handling passengers. Billy could see the lines of freight cars and the maintenance trucks for CSX on the siding.

The town wasn't dying, though. He saw groups of people on both sides of the street. There were black folks talking to white folks, and he saw them laughing and even hugging like they were friends, and he thought how much things had changed in that respect.

The Blue Willow Inn was just up the street on the right. He pulled into the parking lot behind the restaurant. As he walked past the gift shop and up the steps to the front walk, a young lady in a Scarlett O'Hara costume greeted him at the front porch. He gave his name to the hostess in the hallway and went back outside to the porch where the young lady offered him free lemonade and a vacant rocker to pass the time until his table was ready. Billy James sipped on the lemonade and rocked on the porch for about twenty minutes before the hostess touched him on the arm, and then he went inside and followed her to a table.

He got his empty place and quickly found there was no way he could put all the selections on a single plate. He decided to give priority to roast beef, country ham, biscuits, green beans, mashed potatoes, and coleslaw, then come back later for a different course.

It was during the middle of the second helping that he saw somebody that he didn't expect to see ever again, and it made the food stick in his throat. He put his fork down and raised his napkin to his face, and was surprised to find it cold and perspiring.

Billy James could tell the man was watching him although he knew that couldn't be possible. The man hadn't seen him since he became a grown man, and he had been a grown man for a long, long time.

But, there could be no doubt of it. The man was watching him. He got up from his chair. Billy thought he must be at least 95 years old now, but his eyes were as bright and hard as a bobcat's and an odd color of pale green. His skin was stretched over his hawksbill nose and was shiny like the bottom of an old leather chair. The man steadied himself with a cane and began walking between the rows of tables, nodding and smiling here and there to acquaintances. It looked as if the smile was just an incision in his face that revealed nothing of the teeth behind it, and perhaps there were no teeth anyway. The old man was Judge Spencer Vinings Tolliver, unbelievably, still alive.

He was even now with Billy James' table, and he paused long enough to whisper, "Why'd you come back?"

He didn't give time for an answer, even if Billy had come up with one, but went on down the rows and out the big French doors and sat down in one of the vacant rockers.

Billy James saw the man take a glass of lemonade from Miss Scarlett, and he knew he would have to face him. He wished he hadn't turned off the expressway, but he had, and now old Judge Tolliver was out there waiting on the porch. He had to be older even than 95, and he should have been dead long ago, but he wasn't. He was just shriveled up more and meaner looking than the last time he saw him.

Billy pushed his plate away and got up from the table and headed out to the porch. He took a chair next to the old man, and after they sat there for a while, the old man began to rock back and forth very slowly.

"Oh, where have you been, Billy boy, Billy boy, oh where have you been, charmin' Billy?" The old man recited the child's song in a raspy whisper sound, and then he rocked some more. "When your uncle died, and you didn't come to the funeral, I decided that you had pretty good sense after all," the old man said.

"I was in Viet Nam when my uncle died," Billy replied.

"I don't care why you came back," he said finally. "It's too late to bother me, and it won't help anybody or anything for you to talk about what happened. What good can it do to dig up the past?"

"I don't know what I had in mind," Billy said. "I didn't expect to see you, that's for sure."

"I guess you didn't," the old man cackled, "I guess you didn't...but here I am anyway...for what good it does anybody. I guess the good Lord left me for a purpose, but I haven't figured out why."

"Maybe he wanted you to say you're sorry," Billy James said. "Even George Corley Wallace said he was sorry."

"Not 'til hell freezes over," the old man said.

"You might ought to be thinking about hell," Billy James said.

"Well, that was a figure of speech. I don't think much about hell because I never spent much time worrying about fantasy. I think about reality, the here and now of things, and I'll bet you're wondering how I recognized you back there in the restaurant."

"It did puzzle me some," Billy James said.

"The price of fame," the judge replied. "Saw your picture in one of the papers right after you came home from Viet Nam. Lieutenant Billy James Bradley returns home to Augusta, it said. Former Georgia football star and all that. I kept all your newspaper clippings from the Georgia days."

"I guess you spent a lot of time wondering just when I might expose you," Billy James said.

"Nah, I didn't worry too much. I believe in family ties, and I knew you weren't likely to expose your Uncle Joe Bradley or embarrass the family that way. As I say, what good would it do?'

"I guess I just find it hard to believe that 15 or 20 men could kill four other human beings and nobody even got arrested or indicted."

"It was a different time, Billy James. You have to understand that. It was a different time."

Chapter 31

The staff of the Blue Willow Inn had begun clearing the tables in the various dining rooms and the customers had dispersed to the grounds and the gift shop. The judge and Billy James still sat in the rockers on the porch.

"I agree that it was a different time," Billy said,"but I'd like to know something. Has time made any difference at all in the way that you feel about what happened back there?"

The judge took a while to answer. He lifted a gnarled leg with the help of his right hand and crossed it over the other leg. "Not for me," the judge said. "Certainly not for me. I did what was necessary at the time and I haven't changed my mind on it. Given all the circumstances, I don't see how it could have been handled any differently."

"But the LAW judge, -you just forgot about the legality of the thing-took matters into your own hands and deprived four human beings of life. You don't see how that could have been handled differently?"

"You were not a student of the law, were you, Billy James Bradley?" The judge's blue-green eyes bored into Billy James. "No? Well I was, you see. I studied the law and I enforced the law and by God, I WAS the law." The judge nodded his head vigorously and repeated, "Yessir, by God, sir, I WAS THE LAW.

Law is a perverse thing, Billy James. Ignorant people often create laws. Self-serving politicians often use the law for their own selfish interests. The law can be used to protect the guilty or to harm the innocent. The law can be tampered with, Billy James. Sometimes justice has no part in it at all. I could not be tampered with you see."

"But there were others, Judge, two other people that had no hand in the fight or the attempted rape. What was the justice for them?"

"They were in the wrong place at the wrong time. Nobody can be protected from that you see. Spencer, Jr., couldn't be protected from that. Being in the wrong place at the wrong time is an act of God, so to speak." He nodded again, but not as vigorously, as if he was walking over some new ground. "You see...Darnelle...you didn't meet Darnelle, did you?"

"No," Billy James said. "Who is Darnelle?"

The judge paused a moment and ignored the question. "Well, my two boys both went on to higher education. Spencer, Jr. studied agriculture, and he took over the farming, and young Michael...I always called him Mikey...well, he studied textile engineering, and he took over the cotton mill. He sold out to Arondale Mills, you know.

"I didn't know that," Billy said.

"Well, Spencer, Jr. studied agriculture, and he would have inherited the land, would have carried on for the Tollivers, if he had lived."

"What happened?" Billy asked.

"The war," the judge said, "the Korean War. He had gotten his officer's bars in ROTC at Georgia, and they couldn't wait to call him up. Sent him off to Ft. Sill, Oklahoma, and then on to Korea. He was a forward observer...I think they called them. He was so far forward he got killed by his own artillery...friendly fire, they call it now."

The judge closed his eyes, and Billy James waited, wondering if he had dozed off or if he had just finished talking. "But we were talking about Darnelle, weren't we?" The judge opened his eyes and looked at Billy James.

"Well, you asked if I had met her."

"She became an opera singer," the judge said. "The papers said she was another Marian Anderson. I don't know. I never saw one of her performances. She came to see me once. Did you know that?

"No, I didn't"

"Yes, she came to see me...let's see...it must have been in the fifties, about 1956, I'd say. Came all the way out here in one of those hired limousines."

Almost on cue, a limo passed slowly by the Blue Willow and pulled into the parking lot behind the restaurant.

"I suppose she shouldn't have bothered," the old man said. "We didn't hit it off very well. She asked about the boys...Mikey had already sold out and gone to Alaska, and, of course, Spencer had been killed, so she didn't get to see either of them. I guess they were the only reason she would come all that way."

"But, who was she?" Billy asked.

The judge shifted in his chair and reached inside his coat pocket. He brought out a yellowed newspaper article and placed it on the arm of the rocker. Billy James could see it was a picture. He reached for the paper, and then he drew in his breath.

"I SAW this lady once," he said. "I was in California, and I went to the Hollywood bowl. She was the featured soloist, but she didn't call herself Darnelle."

"No, she didn't," the judge replied. People all over the world knew her by this stage name." He retrieved the clipping and chuckled. "I often show this to strangers here on the porch...tell them this was my daughter. it seems to impress them."

"Was she your daughter?" Billy asked.

"All those years," the judge said. "All those years I kept an account open for her…" the judge shook his head, "Yes, you might not think I would go to the trouble, but I kept her account open at the Trust Company. She used it extensively at first when she was getting her schooling at Julliard and when she moved to Paris, but then the money started rolling in, especially after she married the Frenchman…Pierre Fontenot, of the Fontenot Vintners."

"So, was she your daughter?" Billy asked again.

"Hell yes…well of course she was my daughter. She was my illegitimate, half-breed daughter, the child of my Negro house-keeper. She never came back to this country again. She didn't think too much of the United States back then."

"How about today?"

"Oh, she passed away in 1985. Oh yes, I gave Spencer's share to Darnelle. I could have given it all to Mikey, but I didn't. He had all he needed, and besides, he never cared for the land any-way. Didn't care too much for me either, I suppose." The judge fell silent again.

"Anyway, Mikey took his money and moved up to Alaska, and as far as I know, he still lives up there. He has never written to me." The old man shook his head again. "I guess you could say I lost everybody I ever cared about…a punishment from God, some might say, but I don't think that way. So, Darnelle's son, Jacques Fontenot, everybody calls him Jack around these parts, became the inheritor of Mulberry Farms. He divides his time between the vineyards in France and the vineyards at Mulberry Farms. He's over there right now."

"And where do you live?" Billy James asked.

"The same place," the judge said. "The house where my fa-ther was born and his father before him. I'll live there until I die, and then Spencer can have it too."

"I thought you said Spencer died in the Korean War."

"Not my son, but my great-grandson, Spencer Vinings Fontenot."

"I'm surprised to hear you say that."

"That he can have my house?"

"No, that he can have your name."

"Well, that was Darnelle's idea. She knew that she had gotten Spencer's share, don't you see, and so really, I guess her grandson was named for him."

"Do you see him often?"

The judge nodded. "He's about fifteen years old now. Comes over here with Jack when he's not in school. He likes the Georgia soil, compares it to his province and just thinks America is a great place to be. He'll make a good farmer."

"How will he be accepted?"

"He'll be the biggest landowner in Bogart County, Georgia. Folks respect the land barons, you know."

"Yes, I know," Billy James said.

The chauffeur unfolded a wheelchair from the interior of the limo and pushed it up the inclined walkway.

"It's funny how things work out," the judge said. "It used to be against the law to make alcoholic beverages in Georgia. Now we're providing employment and the Mulberry Wine label is an important Georgia export."

The judge placed his bony hands on the rocker arms and pushed himself upward from the chair. Immediately, the chauffeur was alongside to guide him into the wheelchair.

"I guess you'd have to say that it all depends on how you look at a thing," he said. He settled himself into the wheelchair and turned his blue-green eyes back to Billy James.

"It all depends on when you look at a thing," he said. "What looks bad at one time can look all right at another time, and maybe something that looked all right at one time can look somewhat different at another time."

"I cannot imagine," Billy James said, "that what happened back there...could ever look right to anybody at any time."

"It was a DIFFERENT time," the judge said, and he dismissed Billy James with a wave of his hand, and the chauffeur wheeled him toward the car. He looked back as he entered the limo and pointed a bony finger in Billy James' direction. Just in case the chauffeur had paid any attention to the conversation, he explained it for him.

"These Yankee tourists" he cackled, "are always fighting the Civil War with me."

"I'll bet you always win," the chauffeur said.

"I have so far," the judge answered.

Chapter 32

He woke to sunlight stabbing through the slanted blinds of the motel room. He hadn't slept well, and it wasn't just because the mattress was lumpy. The dreams came back again, and at 3 o'clock in the morning, he was drenched in perspiration. He showered and changed into fresh pajamas and got out the Flannie Flagg novel he hadn't found time to read. Somewhere between the pages of *Fried Green Tomatoes*, he fell asleep.

He had breakfast at "Simply the Best Café," a delightful little restaurant on the main street. He ordered ham and eggs with grits and biscuits. The hot food and coffee helped restore his mind and body to the new day at hand.

A big, dappled gray horse was pulling a carriage full of tourists, and they waved and smiled at him. He waved back. He walked along the sidewalks by the furniture stores and the food market, turned the corner and saw the art gallery directly ahead.

The owner, who was also the artist responsible for some of the exceptional paintings lining the gallery walls, invited him to make himself at home and to call him "Bill." The scenes of the Carolina low country and historic buildings along the Georgia coast were outstanding.

After browsing the gallery, he crossed the street to the City Hall and inspected the lobby. Someone had donated two framed pictures of the local cotton mill personnel during the 1940's. He noticed there were no black faces in the group pictures.

He finished his tour at the Sycamore Street Neighborhood Grill. The restaurant was housed in what had been a cotton warehouse. It had beautiful heart pine timbers that contrasted delightfully with the darkened old brick walls. He thought about the old City Café that had been the only "eating out" place when he was here last. Back then, you had country fried steak or hamburger steak with collard greens and mashed potatoes, and cornbread, and banana pudding or fruit cobbler for dessert. Here, there were new things like chicken wings and quesadillos. He chose the latter and found them to be excellent.

He knew he was stalling, putting off the absolute necessity of driving on to Mulberry, and so he got in the car and headed north. Twenty minutes later he crossed into Bogart County, and the change was immediately apparent. Today, the fence lines were free of vines and weeds and the fencing itself was made of plastic. Plastic boards and plastic posts gleamed in their whiteness, and row upon row of grapevines adorned the landscape. The trellis supports for the grapevines wound out of sight and over the hills as far as his eyes could see.

The fencing became sculpted stone, and a huge sign advertised the Mulberry Winery. He parked alongside the arched columns that supported the entrance gate. He could see the mansion through the magnolias lining the drive, the lawn postcard green and the white columns gleaming. He parked the car and took it all in.

There had been sunlight on that day in 1945. There was dew on the cotton plants when he and the dog had set out to pick blackberries. The cotton plants were so large they covered the red soil beneath and the cotton bolls were ripening in the sun.

Then, something bad happened. The bad thing took away his Mulberry summer, and it took the lives of four people riding in a red Hudson automobile. The only good thing that came of the summer was the dog, Lectric. His Uncle Joe had given the dog to him when he drove Billy James back to his Mama. He had ridden with the dog and with Uncle Joe and his dark secrets all the way back to Augusta.

He never talked with anyone about the killings. Not any real person, but he did talk to the dog. The last time they talked the dog was very old and suffering. Billy told him the secret they had shared had been a big burden and he appreciated the fact that Lectric had listened when he couldn't talk to anyone else. Lectric kind of whimpered and licked his hand, and Billy felt he understood.

He sat for a long time remembering. Then, he started the car and turned toward the Appalachee River. He knew he had to physically be there, however much he dreaded the act. He drove slowly along the road to the bridge remembering the boy and the dog and the blackberries and then the bridge came into view and a wave of nausea hit him. He pulled over to the side of the road and retched into the grass until the dry heaves became sobs.

Billy James Bradley cried then. He cried for the father he never got to know and for his mother who had loved him. He cried for the lost lives torn from the earth and he cried for the young boy and the little dog named Lectric and he cried for the lost Mulberry summer.

He didn't know how long he stayed at the bridge. He was no longer conscious of the time. His mind was back there in 1945, and the images he could never erase came flooding back as they had all these years. Nobody ever knew of the dreams that haunted him in the late hours of the night. He would see the rag doll figures of two women lying on the ground with their hands reaching out and the shredded face of the man so close to his hiding place. Often, he would cry out in his sleep, and his mother would wake him and ask if he was hurting. He would always say no. He was a victim of the carnage at the river. It had robbed him of the innocence of youth and had almost cost him his sanity.

The sheriff's car brought him back to reality. He saw it in his rearview mirror, and his stomach immediately tightened as it always did in the presence of a lawman. He supposed it was the guilt he felt by association with the dark secret that he had kept for Uncle Joe. All the people who did the killing were probably dead by now, except for the judge.

Billy knew that the killers were influenced by the judge, but they were also victims of their own fears. They sensed a change coming, and they were afraid. That's why the great silent majority just kept quiet. There were no impassioned pleadings from the pulpits or the newspapers for justice. They kept it quiet.

What was it the judge had said? "It was a different time, Billy James. You have to understand that."

And what was it his Ma used to say? "Listen to me, son. There'll come a day when everything will work out right. You may think it ain't never coming, but God will find a way."

The sheriff's car passed him, and he watched it move on down the road. He started his own vehicle and accelerated a little and kept the sheriff's car in sight. He saw the new Texaco station down on the right. He saw the sheriff pull into a parking space in front of the station and he pulled into the next available spot.

He knew that he had felt guilty for too long a time. There was a need to talk to someone, and suddenly he began to talk to the dog that was no longer there. It just came naturally, talking to the dog.

"Those men at the river...they didn't speak for me," he said.

"They didn't speak for me either," he said for the dog.

"I guess Ma was right," Billy James Bradley said, "about there coming a day. This might be the day when things begin to come right."

"You never know," he said for the dog. "You just never, ever know."

The sheriff came out of the Texaco place. He had a cold drink cup in his hand. He nodded toward Billy James and Billy nodded back. Billy got out of his car and walked toward the sheriff.

"I need to tell you something," he said.

The D.A. was named Lawson Smith, and he was a pleasant chap with prematurely gray hair and a thin, athletic body. Billy was sure he had been a basketball player.

He listened quietly to Billy's story and at the conclusion he walked over and put a hand on Billy's shoulder. "The folks in this community have waited a long time for this," he said. "You will be needed when, and if, this thing comes to trial stage."

Billy James assured him that he would be available. He gave his home address in California and his cell phone and residence phone and told the D. A. that he planned to spend a week or so in the area before he made the long trip back to the West Coast.

He spent the week re-visiting old sites and marveling at the new attractions. He went to the Cyclorama and to the High Museum. He drove the entire distance around the perimeter expressway and found every inch of it developed into shopping centers and subdivisions.

He spent most of his time at the Stone Mountain Inn. He rode the cable car to the top of the mountain, which was advertised to be the largest chunk of exposed granite in the world. He investigated the method used to carve the Confederate generals into the face of the mountain and learned it was done with torches that burned a mixture of kerosene and air. The heat spalled the stone away from the prepared design. In the evening he attended the laser light show, which was projected on the mountain face and then watched the spectacular fireworks display that ended the show.

The telephone call from the D.A.'s office reached him just after breakfast, the following week. His bag was packed and lying on the bed at the Inn and he had just called for a cab.

"Mr. Bradley?"

"Speaking."

"This is Lawson Smith."

"Oh, yes, how're you doing today?"

"I'm facing less work today than yesterday at this time."

"Really? And how might that be?"

"Well, it seems that Judge Spencer Tolliver will not be coming to trial." There was a long pause, and Billy James was thinking that the old scoundrel had won again and then the D.A. came back on the line.

"Spencer Vinings Tolliver died this morning of natural causes, according to Bob Roller at the Coroner's Office."

"I guess he had the last laugh after all," Billy said.

"No, I believe the Devil had the last laugh this time."

ISBN 155369092-3